D1799147

Kev Carter

Back into Darkness

Copyright

ISBN:

978-1-4477-9524-7
Kev Carter

CHAPTER 1

The earthquake had been the biggest England had ever known. It was not very strong in terms of the earthquakes of the world, but for England it was huge. Slates were shaken from roofs, chimney stacks cracked and collapsed, and people were shaken out of their beds. People talked about it for days. The local newspapers showed the damage it had done to houses and buildings.

Amber was fifteen years old and had been having terrible nightmares. Her mother had not paid much attention to them, mind you, she didn't pay much attention to much these days. She was shadow of her former self, overweight, drank too much, smoked too much and was generally unapproachable.

Tommy, Amber's brother, was the one who took notice of her horrid dreams. She dreamt of the terrible time they had gone through at a farmhouse five years earlier. It had left a terrible scar on all their minds. Diane, their mother, could not handle it and had gone downhill ever since.

Tommy had moved away and gone to university, but Amber was still at home and was the one who was affected by it all the most. The earthquake shook her from her bed and she cried for help, frightened. Her mother came in and hit her across the face, told her to stop being so childish and left. It was Tommy who she turned to.

It was Tommy who she wanted to take her back to the place where it started, to see if she could confront the nightmare she was having and somehow suppress it. If she saw the place gone, the emptiness that was left, then maybe she could lay to rest her demons and get on with her life.

Tommy knew their mother would never consent, but he wanted to help his sister so he agreed. He picked her up and they went for the long drive to the farmhouse, or where the farmhouse used to be. None of them had been back since, though none of them would ever forget what happened there. They had never told the whole truth because no one would ever have believed them.

Tommy drove steadily and they didn't say much for about half an hour. Amber suddenly started to talk and said what they both were thinking.

"Whatever happened to Ray, do you know?"

"I have kept tabs on him and I think I have an idea where he is. My friend is a whiz on the internet and you would be amazed at what you can find out with just a little information."

"Was it all his fault? Mum said it was, she is very bitter." Amber glanced over at Tommy who quickly returned the look.

"I don't know, Amber, I don't know." He shook his head and tried not to remember the most terrifying time of his life.

"I don't know what I would say to him now, if I ever saw him again, that is."

"Well, we will probably never see him again, will we?"

"No, probably not. Thank you for bringing me here, Tommy. I have to see the place, to know it is not there for real and it's all only in my mind."

"I want to make sure you can get these demons out of your head and get on with your life, grow up normally and put it all behind you."

"I am trying, but it is very hard. I just cannot forget and the memories will just not leave me alone," she said, her voice becoming distressed. She sat up in her seat and looked out of the window having a moments thought to herself.

Tommy glanced over at her. He could see the torture in her face and hear the fear in her voice. He opened his mouth to say something, then closed it again, unable to think of anything constructive or helpful.

They drove in silence until they were very close to the place and they both started to recognise things, like the pub and the shops. Tommy eased the car steadily up the turning to the road that led up to the house. He stopped and turned to Amber, who was already looking at him with a hint of panic in her eyes.

"Okay, are you sure you want to do this?" he asked her.

"I think I have to, Tommy. Yes, I have to."

Tommy looked her deep in the eye and saw the fear, but he also saw the determination and desperateness she was holding. He gave her a reassuring smile and started to drive up the road.

The last time they were here they were racing down it in Ray's Sierra for their very lives. Both of them could feel their hearts beating faster. Both of them swallowed because of a dry throat and both of them sighed as they reached the pillars where the two gates used to be.

Slowly Tommy turned and pulled into the courtyard. It was empty and desolate; the house was gone, the place dead. The lake loomed in the back but seemed so far away. The whole area was like a no-man's land.

Stopping where the front door used to be, Tommy looked around, beginning to feel a little more at ease. After all, there was nothing here, only his memories of the nightmare, something that would never leave any of them.

The silence was a little unnerving. They could hear nothing, no birds, no slight hum of traffic in the distance, nothing.

Taking a big deep breath, Tommy looked at Amber then opened the door and got out of the car. He hesitated momentarily, pushing himself to get his foot on the ground. Once he had done that, he got out and stood up, looking out across the field and far away into the distance. Turning, he looked back towards the gates, knowing that the woods were that way.

Amber got out of the car tentatively, looking over at Tommy.

"There is nothing here, Amber, nothing left," Tommy told her. He took a deep breath, trying to show her that there was nothing to worry about, but he was not too convincing. The look on his face and little quaver in his voice gave him away, though she appreciated his effort and gave him a little smile.

"Let's walk about, let me see it has all gone."

They both held hands and slowly walked around the ground where the house once stood. Looking down at the calm, still lake, they remembered the horrible creatures that came from there and attacked the house. Tommy held his sister's hand tightly, reassuringly.

Amber looked back up towards the where the two barns were and moved off towards there. Tommy followed, constantly scanning the area. He had become a little uneasy and felt like he was being watched. He put it down to nerves and apprehension.

The two barns were gone, just like everything else, not even the rubble was left. Standing where the main doors would have been, Amber looked in and remembered herself being excited the first time she came here.

"I don't think I would have ever gotten my pony, would I?"

"Probably not, no." Tommy walked past her towards the end of the clearing where he noticed a small mound on the uneven ground. He walked towards it, stopping short and pulling back a little at the smell coming from it.

"What is it?" Amber asked, seeing his reaction.

"I'm not sure. A burst sewer, I think." Tommy went closer, moving upwind of the odor. Amber rushed over and held onto his arm, looking down at the ground. The crack in the earth was clearer to see from this angle. It was like a dark, gaping wound, emitting an obnoxious stink.

"This must have been under the barns when they were still here. I wonder what it is." Tommy leaned forward a little to try and see inside the black hole below them.

"Careful, Tom, it might be dangerous."

He bent down and pulled a large piece of grass off the side and it revealed a circle of stone. He cleared more rubble away and pulled back now and again as the smell caught his nostrils when he came too close.

Finally he was left with a sight that looked like it had been covered for centuries and probably was. A circle of stone like a seal, packed and forged into place. A large crack had broken across it and some of the stones were now loose. Tommy looked up at Amber, who backed off nervously.

Without saying a word, he knelt down and pulled at one of the stones, finding it was stuck fast. He reached over and tried another one; this one gave under his tug and came free. He tried a second one and then a third. Soon he was left with a hole big enough to get into.

He stood, suddenly panicking, not knowing why he was doing what he was doing.

"What do you think it was?" Amber asked.

"I don't know. It's so dark in there, why isn't the light shining in and making it so we can see inside?"

They both looked up at the sun beating down on them and then down at the hole. The light seemed to stop at the edge of the hole and it went no further.

"Let's go, I don't like this," Amber said.

Tommy looked at her and then down at the hole, shaking his head. He agreed with her, he did not like it either, it made him nervous.

"Is there anything else you want to see or do, Amber, now that we are here? I want you to be free of whatever is troubling you. You can see the whole place is gone and nothing is left; no house, no demons, nothing."

"Just a hole in the ground," she said, looking at it again.

"Yes, but we are both nervous here, so we are probably reading too much into this. It is just a sewer or something, nothing at all." He tried to convince his sister by convincing himself.

She smiled at him and looked around the place once again at the desolation, the emptiness, the quiet.

"It's dead, isn't it? The evil that was here has killed this bit of land, this bit of the earth is dead." she said, her head up, listening to the silence.

"Yes and we were very lucky. It is over now and will never return to hurt us again. Whatever it was or wherever it came from, it will never hurt us again."

Looking back at him, she nodded and smiled. Her smile froze, however, and began to change into a grimace as she felt the slight tremor under her foot. She looked down and saw the crack in the ground coming from the hole. Silently but steadily the earth was opening beneath her feet.

Tommy looked down, but before either of them could do anything, it was too late. The hole opened and Amber was gone. She dropped like a man from the gallows straight down into the earth. The stench made Tommy heave and he put his hand over his mouth.

Peering into the blackness, he couldn't see or hear anything.

"Amber, Amber, are you all right?" he shouted, hearing no response.

He dropped to one knee and looked into the impenetrable darkness below him. His heart was pounding with dread, his mouth was dry with panic and his eyes were wide with fear.

He let out a scream as the two hands shot out of the darkness at him, looking as though they were reaching up to the sky. He backed off slightly, vibrating with fear. He rubbed his eyes and his mouth dropped open involuntarily as he saw his sister float up from the dark recess she had fallen into.

She stood by the side of the hole silently. She seemed calm and collected as she stared at her brother.

He swallowed hard and stood up, never taking his eyes from her as she gazed at him. He looked down into the hole, where he noticed the a of light now shining into the hole, unlike before.

Amber stood stiffly, slowly turning her head to gaze at the surroundings as she took deep breaths of air into her lungs.

"Are you all right, Amber, is everything okay?" Tommy asked uncertainly.

"Kaden. Where is Kaden?" she asked in a lower tone of voice than her own. Her intense gaze was piercing and it made her brother uneasy.

He rubbed his mouth with the back of his hand nervously. He shook his head, not understanding her question.

"Amber, are you all right? What is wrong?" he said, beginning to shake and worry.

"Amber? Yes, Amber is fine. Can we go from this place?" she said in her normal voice.

He nodded and led her back to the car. They both got in and he drove away. She did not speak again and so nothing else was said for at least an hour. Looking at her occasionally as he drove, Tommy felt very uneasy. She was not right, she was too quiet. She looked calm, but he could feel that something was not right.

"You didn't hurt yourself, did you? Bang your head or anything like that?" he asked her.

She ignored his question, looking at the passing scenery with confusion.

"Where is Kaden? I want to meet him," she said again, without looking at Tommy.

"Who is this Kaden?" he asked.

She grinned an evil grin that sent a shiver down his spine. She stared at him, her eyes burning into him, staring into his very mind.

He began to feel the pressure in his skull and he shook his head, trying to break free of this grip that seemed to be holding him from within his brain. It eased and stopped as Amber turned and looked out of the window again. They drove in silence the rest of the way.

CHAPTER 2

Ray was sitting in his chair, looking out the window, with Bodie laying next to him. Both looked bored, both wanted to be somewhere else.

"How many jobs is that now, Ray?" Chris said in annoyance as she came from the kitchen with two mugs of tea and a packet of biscuits under her arm.

She gave the biscuits to Ray with a mug of tea and she sat across from him, looking at him for an answer.

Ray opened the biscuits and dunked one in his tea saying, just before he put it in his mouth, "I'm not sure. A couple?"

"It's six, Ray. Bloody six jobs you have now had and lost in eighteen months." Her voice was questioning and irritated.

"I am not taking shit like that from a wanker like that. He is lucky I didn't break his fucking jaw."

"He was your boss, Ray. Get in the real world. That is what it is like, you go to work, you get told what to do, and you get paid. Bite your tongue and just get on with it, that is what the rest of the country has to do."

"It's shit and I don't see why some little fucker who doesn't know his arse from his elbow can come to me and tell me what the fuck he wants. He has no idea what the hell he is on about, he's never even done the job, but he is there talking to me like a piece of shit." He took a gulp of his tea and two more biscuits disappeared.

"It is called the way of the world. I have told you before, you will have to adjust, love. People will piss you off, especially at work, but you have to bite your tongue and just bow your head and let it ride. The more you rear up to them, the more they will do it."

"He's lucky he is still fucking walking straight, the little twat," he said, looking at Chris for the first time.

"And to be honest, Ray, you are lucky you have not been arrested and prosecuted. You cannot say these things to people, you cannot keep threatening your managers or the other people above you because you just lose your job like you have today." She shook her head and sighed at him in frustration.

"I'm not going to say sorry for taking shit from a little wanker who is above his station and wants taking outside and taught a lesson."

"I knew you would find it hard to adapt, I mean, what you have seen and been through, who wouldn't? But Ray, you are no better now than you were a year ago. How long is it going to take, love?" Her voice was not so much pleading as demanding and Ray picked up on her distress instantly.

"I don't know, maybe if I left for a while?"

"I don't want you to fucking leave, I want you to settle, be normal and get on with your life, our life." Her voice was raised and she had an annoyed tone.

Bodie pricked his ears up and sat up looking at Ray; he could sense what was coming.

"I am sorry I am not able to be the perfect little partner you want, Chris. Yes sir, no sir, whatever you want sir, it is not me. I have never been able to just shut my mouth and say nothing, I say what I like and like what I say. A Yorkshire man, that's me," he said, convinced that what he said explained everything.

"Oh, get out of your own arse, Ray. You are living in this world, man, you can't have that attitude anymore, you won't last ten minutes, for Christ's sake." She stood up and shook her head at him, then walked over to the window and looked out at nothing in particular.

"Maybe I should write a book," he said, looking at her back as she stared out into the street below her.

Turning, she looked at him, his blue eyes fixed on her. She remembered all that they had been through. She saw the warrior she loved, but the man needed to get into the real world. She thought she would have be able to do it by now, but it was apparent that it was going to be much harder than she thought.

"I have some time off, shall we go to France? I want to do some research into Angelique and I feel that is where she originated. It would be a nice break for us and we will be away from here for a while."

"France? Why didn't you just ask her what you wanted to know when you saw her face to face?"

He had missed the whole point and she gave up there and then. She was about to let loose the built-up anger, but was stopped when Bodie stood upright and growled. They knew someone was approaching.

Moments later, a tentative knock came to the door and Bodie barked until Ray lifted his hand to silence him.

Chris walked to the door and opened it. Her face was like thunder and she had no idea who this young man was who looking at her so nervously.

"Does Ray Sibson live here please?" he said.

"Who wants him and why?" she snapped.

"My name is Tommy and I used to know Ray some years ago when he dated my mum. I have need of his assistance and would appreciate it if you could let me know where he lives." Tommy looked desperate and he was.

"Wait here," Chris said, walking back into the room.

Tommy took a deep breath and found himself shaking a little. he thought he would never see Ray again and it made him uneasy thinking that he might now. He knew Ray never really liked him anyway, so why would he be different when he sees him again.

Chris came back moments later and gestured him inside. He carefully walked in and followed Chris to the main room. His anxiety rose as he first saw Bodie staring at him, then he saw Ray standing in the middle of the room, staring intensely and curiously at him.

"Ray, how are you?" Tommy said quietly as he stopped dead at the sight of him. His knees were weak and he had to pull himself together, taking a deep breath.

Ray nodded, saying nothing as Chris sat down.

The atmosphere was uneasy and Tommy didn't really know what to say and dreaded the reaction he would get.

"Have you something to say?" Chris asked him, looking up at him as she sat back in her chair.

"Yes. Yes, I have. I need your help and hope you will be able to save my sister. Ray, I have no one else to turn to."

"How the fuck did you find me?" was Ray's only concern at this time.

"I have very good friends who can find anyone with just a little information. The internet is an amazing and useful thing if you know how to access the right things."

"How the fuck did you find me?" Ray repeated the question.

"You weren't hard to follow, Ray, if you look in the right places. Any trouble or mysterious unsolved things you leave a wake in your wake. I don't understand how the hell you never got caught. I did lose track of you for some time, but then you registered your car at this address with the DVLA. We can get someone's address just by telling them they were illegally parked and they will supply you with the address of the owner of the car. You have to know how to do it, of course, and like I said, I have good friends at university."

"What the fuck are you on about?" Ray had already lost patience.

"It doesn't matter, I just found you, okay?" He backed off a little physically as well as verbally when he saw the anger rise in Ray and he stepped forward.

"Listen, lad, I have had enough of mouthy little wankers for one day, so piss or get off the pot. I have better things to do than talk over old times with you. What the fuck do you want and why are you here?"

"Do you know who Kaden is?" Tommy asked, looking Ray in the eye for his reaction.

Ray held still and covered it well, giving nothing away, as did Chris. Tommy did not realise it, but from this moment on he had their undivided attention.

"Why not look it up with your good friends on the fucking internet?" Ray told him.

"I have. He was a witch finder, a killer and a destroyer of evil. He lived centuries ago."

"So what do you want me for?"

"Amber is in a bad way and my mum is a nervous wreck. I think you can help. And I think it's got something to do with the old farmhouse. Something is still alive out there. Will you help us, please Ray? There is no one else I can turn to."

"Why do you think something is happening out there again?"

"Amber been having horrible nightmares, dreams of the farmhouse and horrid visions. She wanted to go and investigate so I took her back there. We saw nothing at first, just a wasteland, then we discovered this well-type of hole. It was cracked and broken, it must have been hidden under one of the barns or something. Anyway, it looked like it had been sealed and now it was broken, possible the earthquake we had, I don't know. As we investigated, Amber lost her footing and fell in. When she got back out, she was strange and silent. It scared me, Ray, it was not right. Something was very wrong. I thought she had knocked her head or something and maybe got a concussion. Then she asked for Kaden.

"When I got her back to Mum's, that is when it all started. She started to act odd and got violent and worse. It's so bad now we had to restrain her, Ray." He looked worried and Chris watched him and could feel he was telling the truth; he was genuinely scared.

"What did this well or whatever it was look like?" she asked him.

"It was a circle of stone looked like it had been forged together but there was a crack in it and it had broken open"

He preferred looking at her, as Ray's stare was upsetting him. He had always been scared of Ray and he was even more so now.

"Did you see any sign of a seal on it, any markings?"

"No, I didn't, but there might be some. I don't know."

"Was there anything else strange that you noticed, anything at all? Think, son, and think bloody hard."

"It smelt putrid and I noticed there was no light penetrating the darkness. It was sunny, but the hole was black as if the light could not get into it." He shook his head in confusion, worried that he sounded stupid.

Chris thought he was far from stupid; she could see he was telling the truth and could hear the fear in his voice. She bit her bottom lip as she thought, then looked at Ray. She could see the memories and thoughts racing through his head.

Standing, she stood in front of Ray and gave him a cautious look, then she turned to Tommy.

"Give us a little time, son. Leave your address and telephone number"

"I don't know who else to turn to or what to do," Tommy pleaded as he took a little notebook and pen from his inside jacket pocket.

As he wrote in this and pulled a page out, Chris gave Ray a stare. she saw the intense look on his face and needed to talk to him, but alone.

Taking the page with the information she asked for from Tommy, she showed him out. Ray said nothing to him as he left. Chris came back into the room and saw Ray had gone back in time. He seemed the same as when she first met him; the warrior was back and all the work she had tried to do in the past two years was lost. Her man would never

be able to adapt to this world; he was a fighter, a hunter of evil, and now he had
something else to hunt. He had come back to life.

CHAPTER 3

"Ray, think before you act. Let's just talk this through first. Sit down and we will
discuss it," Chris told him as she walked back up to him.

He looked at her and then Bodie for a moment. She thought he was going to leave
and just go on his way. But he didn't. He turned and looked down at her standing close to
him.

"I will never be free of it, Chris. I'll never be able to just walk away from it."

"Listen, if they have released something, then we must try and find out what it is.
I would like to go and look at the place, see it for myself, then we might have a better
idea what we are dealing with. It sounds like something had been sealed in there and now
it has escaped and is asking for Kaden. It must be something you tried to destroy or
maybe Angelique entombed whatever it is. We have to be careful, especially now. I think
we should look at the cards and the board, ask questions."

"You didn't want to touch them again. You said we have got to move on and lead
a normal life."

"I know, but this is not normal, is it? We have to be prepared and get as much
help as we can, we cannot just ignore it. Whatever it is will come for you, that is for sure,
and if it is coming for you, then it is coming for me too."

Ray took a deep exaggerated breath, knelt down and then held his dog in a hug
while he stroked his head. He finally looked up at Chris and nodded. She went away and
returned several minutes later with her tarot cards under her arm and the Ouija board in a

black bag she gave to Ray.

She took the cards and held them in her hands, closed her eyes and was still for several moments.

Ray took the board out of the bag and put it on the floor, placing the planchette on the surface. He looked down and the thoughts and memories were there of the times and the dangers he had witnessed with this board and the battles it had lead him into and through.

Chris placed the cards out in front of her, instantly feeling that there was something wrong. Ray could feel nothing; the board seemed dead to him, just a board. He got nothing from it at all. He looked at Chris and could see on her face she was experiencing the same with her cards; they were dead, useless.

Looking at each other then back at the cards and board, a confused look came across both their faces.

"What has happened? Why are they not working? Have we lost the power or something?" Ray asked her, baffled.

"We never will lose the power. I think something is blocking the energy, something doesn't want us to contact...." she stopped as a thought came to her.

"What? What is it, what are you thinking?" Ray insisted on knowing.

"It must be very powerful to be able to intercept the energy. Something so powerful that it could not be killed so it had to be entombed for eternity. The only way it could be stopped was to encase it in the well or whatever it was. The man who could help us we cannot get in touch with, that is why it, whatever it is, is stopping us from using these."

"So it knows where we are then?" Ray asked, already knowing the answer, Chris looked at him without answering, then she packed the cards away.

Ray stood and stretched his arms out, cracking his shoulders and arms. He knew he had a fight on his hands once again. Chris also stood; she was deep in thought once again and her mind was racing. Ray waited, he knew the explanation would come soon.

"If this thing is so powerful, Ray, I think it as been using its power all along. Maybe it was weakened while in the well, but strong enough to control and possess the family who lived in the farmhouse, that is what sent them insane in the first place. They could not get to it because it was sealed. Then when you were there, it tried to destroy you. This girl obviously is the weak link and it has found her and brought her to it. The seal on the well has been broken somehow and it is now free again, but what the hell is it?"

"I will go and kill it, we know where the fucker is." Ray was becoming agitated and anxious to get going again.

"It is not going to be that easy. This is something special if it can block the energy. It is all powerful and will not be easy to find or kill, if in fact it can be killed. You have never come up against anything like this before and I am worried, very worried indeed. There are some friends I would like us to go and see, they might be able to tell us more about what we are up against."

"We don't have time, I want to go and confront the fucker."

"You have to be ready and be aware of what we are up against this time, Ray. This is not just evil, it is beyond evil."

Ray looked at his woman and could she was concerned. He knew it must be very serious for her to be so.

"Let us go and find out. Fuck," he said, just remembering something.

"What is it?"

"My car, it's in bits, isn't it. I have to go and get it sorted. Listen, you go and find your friends or whoever you are going to see. I will fix my car and then we will decide what we are going to do."

"Do you realise how fucking serious and dangerous this is?" She thought it and said it at the same time. It never ceased to amaze her how he accepted the situation and would handle it when it came to him, this is how he fought. She decided to leave it for now and let him kick start his warrior mode while she went and saw some occultist friends.

It was several hours later and Ray was in the motor accessory shop. He had already put his engine back together and just wanted the finishing touches now. He put his oil on the counter, while waiting to be served by a young arrogant looking lad. Ray took an instant dislike to him. Getting any response, he began to get agitated.

"Am I getting served today or what?" he asked sarcastically.

The young lad, in his early twenties, smirked to himself and cockily walked over to Ray, staring him in the eye as he did from. He stood and waited for Ray to speak.

Ray's blood was beginning to boil and he had to calm himself for a moment.

"Spark plugs, distributor cap, rotary arm, oil filter, air filter and brake pads for a Ford Sierra two litre injection on a G plate," Ray said without taking a breath.

The cocky lad looked amused and started to laugh ignorantly before asking, "You are joking. This is a motor accessory shop, not an antique shop, mate. They don't make then old bangers anymore."

"Get me the parts and shut up."

The lad shook his head and opened a drawer under the counter. Taking a book out, he flicked through the pages to Ford, then Sierra. He looked and fingered down the page, shaking his head and trying to stop a giggle.

He turned and looked on the back shelving where most of the parts were. It took him several minutes to find what he was looking for and place them all on the counter.

Ray picked up the distributor cap and held it up.

"This is the wrong one, son."

"No, it's not. That is what it says in the book."

"I want the light brown one, not the black one."

"That is the right one, be told."

"I built the fucking engine from scratch, son, now give me the fucking light brown distributor cap and stop messing me about, you arrogant little shit."

"You can't talk to me like that, who do you think you are?"

"That's just it, son, I know who I am but you have no fucking idea who you are."

"You're just weird." The boy changed the part and rang it all in the till in silence, then muttered the total to Ray who paid in cash.

He got the things in two bags and left the shop, shaking his head at the state of the youth he keeps encountering.

He marched back and started to work on his car instantly; fixing the new parts, changing the oil and generally checking the car over. The main problem he had with it was the rust, but he had been able to keep it in check and catch any bit early. He was proud of his old car and did not take kindly to anyone insulting it.

After he had finished, he cleared the old parts away and cleaned up. He took the car out for a run and satisfied himself it was back to where it should be; the service had made the difference.

He got a shower and, while he was in there, Chris came back in. Ray walked into the room naked and stood dripping on the floor as he heard her return.

"What if I had brought someone back here with me?" Chris asked, looking at his wet naked body admiringly.

"Rather see that than be blind, lass," he replied with a smile. "Did you learn anything?" He pulled a towel off a radiator and stood in front of the window drying himself.

"Ray, come away from the bloody window, for Christ's sake."

He walked into the room with a sigh and waited for an answer to his question while drying himself.

"The friends I spoke to seem to know nothing of this and are all just as mystified as we are. It must go back a long, long way and must be so powerful." She shook her head and sat down in the chair, running her hands through her hair.

"So what is the plan? I think we should go and confront it and see what we are up against," he said rubbing his short hair and then down each arm in turn.

"We have to be careful. This is not just some bloody witch, this is something much more powerful. I am worried and so are my friends, and so should you be. It is asking for you by name." She tried in vain to convey the seriousness of this to him, though she knew she didn't get through.

"Well, we have to confront it sooner or later, don't we?"

He finished drying his body and stood there naked in front of her. She looked up at him and smiled, then nodded. Ray moved off to the bedroom to get dressed.

She watched him go and kept looking at the doorway he had gone through, shaking her head slowly. She glanced down at Bodie, who was looking at her and watching her expressions. Odd, she thought to herself; she was finding Bodie's stare unnerving.

As she stood, she felt a stabbing pain in her side and sat down again in shock. Confused, she waited until the pain subsided and then eased herself upright. She walked into the bathroom and closed the door behind her.

CHAPTER 4

They had packed all they thought they might need into the car and the old weapons had been retrieved from the locked storage in Chris's place. Food, rations, sleeping bags; it was just like old times for Ray.

Chris had noticed a change in him. As soon as the challenge had shown itself, he had kicked back into old mode once again. His life suddenly had purpose and he had something to hunt down and fight.

Chris rang Tommy on her mobile as they were setting off and informed him that they were coming, also telling him not to tell Amber anything, in fact, she instructed him to keep himself and his mother away from her altogether until they arrived.

Ray had some idea where he was going, though he wasn't sure of the entire route. Chris studied the map and sorted them out while Bodie settled on the back seat.

"Wonder what she will do when she sees you?" Chris said.

"It all depends on what it is that is inside her, doesn't it?"

"I meant Diane, not the child," Chris corrected him.

Ray looked over at her for a moment then back out the windscreen before answering her.

"I don't give a shit. I'm not going there for her."

"You must have thought something of her at one time. You set up home with her and took on two kids. I find it so hard to comprehend, knowing you like I do, that you ever considered doing that."

"So do I. It was another time and place. I have learned much since then. I was

24

confused and didn't understand what was happening or the feelings I was having." He sighed and shook his head before continuing.

"I'm now sure of who I am and what I'm doing."

"So nothing is going to be stirred when you see her?"

"Of course not. Chris, you are worth a thousand of her and don't have any doubts about anything like that. It is over and dead with Diane. Looking back, it should never of fucking started, to be honest but, like I said, you live and learn."

"I'm satisfied with that. Just so we know where we stand because I am not taking an ounce of shit from her if she starts."

"I wouldn't expect you to. Give back what you get, love."

"I fucking will, and harder." Chris was defensive and territorial; she was ready to defend her man and God help anyone, man, woman, or beast that tried to stop her.

They were nearing their destination and they consulted the map more and more as they reached the housing estate. It was run down and the families that lived here were all the same; on welfare and unemployed. It was much easier to scrounge off of the state than to work. Both Ray and Chris took an instant disliking to the area as soon as they drove into it.

"I'm glad Bodie is in the car," Ray said as he pulled up to the street and turned the corner looking for the number they needed. The place was rough and you wouldn't want to live here unless you had to.

They stopped in front of the house. The curtains were dirty, the gate was missing and the whole appearance was scruffy. Looking at each other they exchanged a wordless stare.

Looking up, they saw the front door open and Tommy come out. He walked down the two steps and across the concrete path that lead to the street. He stood and waited to greet them as they both got out of the car.

Ray looked around and made mental notes of the area as he was locking his car up and Chris smiled at Tommy.

He returned the smile then looked at Ray with panic in his eyes and swallowed before looking around nervously and speaking in a low tone.

"It's gotten worse. She is so violent now."

"Where is she?" Ray asked. He stood next to Chris and put his arm around her for reassurance.

"We have her in the upstairs back bedroom. We had to tie her up in a chair, she was just so violent."

"Didn't you take her to a doctor or anything?"

"Mum wouldn't let us. She is at her wit's end, Ray, and so am I."

Ray noticed movement at the front door and saw a figure appear there. It was silhouetted, but he knew it was Diane. She had put weight on and did not stand to well, he thought.

Chris was already looking up in that direction and knew she had nothing to worry about instantly.

Ray saw Diane was smoking. It disgusted him; he hated cigarettes and just detested everything about them.

"What do you want to do?" Tommy asked, seeing Ray's distaste.

"We'd better go see her and try to find out what the hell is going on."

Ray walked past Tommy with Chris by his side. Diane moved away and into the house as they walked up the short path and through the front door.

The smell of smoke irritated his nose instantly and he didn't want to be there any longer then he had to be. The place was in need of a thorough cleaning. The paper was peeling off and at one point had been stuck back to the wall with masking tape. Bare furnishings and dirty carpets with ashes and dirt ground in completed the sorry picture.

He walked into the main room and was confronted with a woman he used to know. She was sitting on a torn settee, smoking nervously. Her hand was shaking and she was dragging on the cigarette as if her life depended on it. She had gained stones in weight and looked years older then she was, a shadow of her former self. Ray wondered what he ever saw in her in the first place.

Diane looked up and the hate in her eyes was apparent right from the start. She stared at Ray and blankly looked across at Chris, saying to Ray as she continued looking at Chris, "This is what your shagging now, is it?" Her voice was venomous and hateful; she was bitter and had become twisted with it.

"Yeah, he moved up from the trash league, love," Chris said, holding her stare and standing her own.

"Fuck off, bitch, or I will cut your fucking throat."

"I'm standing here if you want to try it, bitch. You were too stupid to keep hold of him, so tough shit."

"That's enough, for fuck sake." Ray stepped in and stood between them both.

Tommy tried to defuse the situation by saying, "Look we are all here to try and help Amber, not fight amongst ourselves. Come on, let's act our age."

"You shut up," Diane told him as she stood and looked at Ray, "All this is your fucking fault. You have ruined my fucking life."

"Bollocks. You have not got up and moved on. Don't try and put your inadequacies onto me. You had all the insurance and everything, I took nothing, fuck all. You have just become a bitter, twisted old cow."

"Oh, and what have you been doing in the last four years? Fuck all, except shagging that, I suppose." She pointed to Chris with hate in her eyes.

"You left Ray and have regretted it. You can't have him back now, so live with it," Chris added, just to make herself feel better.

Just then a piercing scream came from upstairs, loud enough to make the window glass rattle in the frames. Tommy ran and closed the front door; he didn't want any nosy neighbours investigating. Diane slumped back down onto the settee and took another drag of her cigarette. She looked to the floor, seeming to block out her daughter's shouts from upstairs.

Ray looked at Chris, who in turn was having trouble believing that her man was ever involved with this woman. She satisfied herself that the woman was now damaged goods and in no way would she ever pose a threat to her, not that she ever did.

A low dark menacing voice boomed down from the up stairs room like a powerful force of its own.

"Kaden."

Ray walked out the room and went up the bare wooden stairs, Chris followed and Tommy, frightened and breathing heavily, brought up the rear.

Standing in front of the door, Ray again looked around, familiarising himself with his surroundings. He then turned to Tommy, asking him, "Where is she exactly, and what is in the room?"

"There's nothing much in there; a bed and a wardrobe, that is all. She is in a chair, I had to bind her."

"What sort of chair? And what have you tied her with and how?" Ray wanted to know.

"It's a wooden chair, I have tied her feet to the legs and her wrists behind her back." He had a tear in his eye and was just about holding himself together.

"What is she tied with?"

"Rope. I used nylon rope."

Ray faced the door and put his hand on the handle, turned it and went into the room. The smell of urine and excrement was strong, but he was focused so he didn't let it bother him. He saw Amber tied in a wooden chair just like Tommy had said she was, slumped down and looking as if she were asleep.

Chris came in and stood next to Ray while Tommy stayed out in the hallway, unable to stop himself crying.

Amber was wearing a short dress, though it was filthy now. She stirred on the chair a little then slowly lifted her head. Her eyes were black as coal and when she opened her mouth, this too was black and her tight lips were turning purple. She stared at Ray for a moment then glanced at Chris.

"Kaden and his whore," she said in an excited voice, pulling at her ties and making the veins stick out in her wrists.

Opening her legs, she showed Ray that she was wearing nothing under her short dress. She stuck her tongue out and flicked it from side to side at him.

"Want to fuck little Amber, Kaden?" she asked, in Amber's voice. She smiled and dropped her head to one side, never taking her eyes from his.

"Who are you?" Ray asked.

"You know who I am, Kaden," she roared in a husky voice that was not her's and not of this time.

"I have forgotten, remind me," Ray said in a raised but calm voice. He looked back and forth from the demon in the chair in front of him to Chris.

"You know me and you will know more pain than anyone ever has known, Kaden, you and your whore."

"You don't know who you are, do you?" Ray insisted.

"I am the one you fear, the one you cannot destroy, and you know I will always come back for you."

Amber's eyes changed colour from black to deep red, then pale green then back to black as she stared at Ray intensely. Pulling and straining constantly at the rope around her wrists and feet, she looked like she was squirming about all the time and ready to break free at any moment.

"What is your name and why were you sealed in a well?" Ray asked in a calm voice.

Amber roared with laughter and spat out at Chris without taking her eyes from Ray.

"You don't know, do you? You have forgotten. You cannot look back, can you? You cannot get your help." Dropping her head onto her chest, she giggled and flicked her tongue out once again, letting drips of vile black spittle drop to her legs from her mouth and nose.

"I don't need help to destroy you, because you do not know who you are," Ray said, sounding uninterested.

"It is you who don't know who I am."

"Show yourself then, show me who you are."

"You will see just before I take you down to hell where a vile creature like you will spend eternity."

"Well, that's been tried before and it's not gotten me there yet."

Chris was trying to study this thing in the chair but it was not giving anything away. She had never seen a possession before, though she knew about them and had asked question today about them when she was with her white witch friends.

She wasn't looking for the classic symptoms of possession; speaking in a different language, shows of tremendous strength or a change in features, just some clue as to who this was and why it knew all about Kaden.

"You have come to the end, Kaden." With that, the ropes snapped simultaneously from her hand and feet and she dashed with tremendous power and speed out of the chair towards Ray.

He was more than ready for her. He threw a powerful right straight into her face as she flew for him, knocking her back dazed and shocked.

Chris pounced on top of the girl, grabbing the ropes and with great speed was able to bind her wrists and feet once again, leaving her spitting and squirming on the floor.

Ray looked down at the girl expressionlessly, watching the blood pouring from her nose and seeing her front tooth broken off where he had hit her.

"I will always find you, Kaden, always, and I will toy with you and taunt you until I am ready to destroy you."

With that, the whole room shook and the window shattered as if something was thrown through it from the inside. Silence followed for a split second. Amber then began to sob on the floor; she was herself again, the demon had left her.

CHAPTER 5

Ray looked at Chris, who looked back at him with just as much confusion.

"It doesn't make sense, does it?" he asked her.

Chris stood up straight and watched as Tommy crept into the room and looked at Amber sobbing on the floor. He was crying uncontrollably.

"Tommy, has she ever been like this since the time at the farmhouse?" Chris asked him.

Tommy shook his head to say no, unable to speak.

"Well it's left her, but where the hell as it gone, and will it come back?" Ray asked Chris.

"Why is it not talking in an ancient language, or at least in the old English, if it has been held captive in a well or hole for centuries?" Chris asked him.

"I don't know." he replied with a shrug. "It's left the girl, I just don't know where the fuck it's gone. It knows what I look like now, so it could be in anyone or maybe anything. This just gets better and better."

Chris's face lit up with sudden awareness. "I think it is a darkness shifter." Seeing Ray's confusion, she explained, "It can move from one victim to another. If you kill the host, then it just moves to another, which is why you can not kill it. You are just killing the shell it is possessing, you're not killing the thing itself, the spirit, the entity or whatever this fucker is."

"Why didn't you tell me this before?" Ray wanted to know.

"I didn't know until I saw it. A wizard told me once and when I went to see my friends the white witches this afternoon, they touched on it as an explanation. These things have been around since the beginning of time, and no one seems to know where they came from."

"So how do we destroy the bastard?"

"I have no idea. I would say you cannot destroy it, it is shifter and just moves from one person to another."

"So how was it sealed in the well?"

"I have no idea." Chris shook her head and shrugged her shoulders.

Ray grew agitated. This was not something he was expecting; he wanted an enemy he could hunt and kill, not something that hid behind others.

Tommy looked up at Ray and asked with a tearful voice, "Can I untie her and get her cleaned up?"

Chris nodded to him and helped him untie Amber while Ray went to the window and looked out into the darkening sky across the rooftops of the council estate.

Somewhere out there was this thing, it could be in anyone or anything, watching him, ready to pounce, and he would have no idea who or what it had possessed.

Chris stood next to him and looked out, wondering the same thing. She sighed and breathed deeply of the air coming in the smashed open window, though she wished she hadn't, considering the odour.

"Don't take a lungful of air in a place like this, love," Ray told Chris as he looked down at her.

"Thanks for the warning, though it's too late."

Diane came into the room and stood by the door. Ray spun around on his heels and, for a moment, looked at her curiously. All he could see was just the wrecked bitter woman who use to be the Diane he knew.

"What's happened?" Diane asked, looking at the window.

"Whatever it was has left her, hopefully for good," Ray said, looking past her as Amber came in the room, sobbing and holding some toilet paper to her bleeding nose.

She pushed past her mother and walked up to Ray and Chris. Tommy came in and joined his sister and Ray looked at this family standing in front of him and remembered them when he lived with them. How times had changed them and how time had changed him.

"Come on," he said to Chris, "there is no more we can do here." They both pushed past the children and walked to the door.

Diane was staring at him and asked in a relatively calm and sincere voice, "What happened to you Ray? Why are you so burnt out?"

Ray was going to reply but instead he just pushed past her and walked off down the stairs.

Chris turned to Tommy. "If anything else happens or you remember anything you want to tell me, get in touch."

"Yes, I will. Thank you and thank Ray for me, for us."

Chris looked Diane in the eye and held the stare for a moment. She slowly shook her head in disgust and left.

Ray was in the car waiting when she came out of the house. She walked to the car and got in.

"That's over and done," she said to him.

"I think it has just started. I don't understand what is going on here, it just does not make sense."

"Does it ever make sense? Do we ever really understand what the hell is happening? This is not your everyday occurrence, is it?" Chris said, putting her seatbelt on and taking a last look up at the house. She could see the three occupants at the window looking down.

Ray started his car and pulled away, watched by the makeshift family that once he was a part of but never would be again.

"If it used the girl to find me, does that mean it does not know where I am all the time? Why didn't it just come for me in the first place?" Ray questioned.

"Where are we going?" Chris asked, looking at Ray. She could see he was deep in thought and just driving on remote.

"There must be someone who can help, someone who knows about these things," he said.

"It must be very powerful to be able to stop the energy, to stop us communicating through the cards."

"If it is that powerful, why is there no record of it? Not even folklore."

"There is, I told you, just not enough knowledge on how to destroy it, or if it can be destroyed."

"Someone entombed the fucker once, so it must be able to be caught or controlled."

"Kaden maybe?" She looked at him as he looked at her.

"Does it have to touch the person it possesses, or can it just take them over however it wants?"

"Ray you are asking me questions I do not know the answer to. I have no idea about this thing at all."

"Tomorrow I want to go back to the farmhouse and look around, see where it came from, see if we can find anything we can use. Are you all right with that?"

"I am all right with anything, don't worry about me. I am just as much involved as you, don't forget."

"We will stay somewhere tonight and go tomorrow we'll have a look around and see what is left."

They drove off into the darkening night and, after a few hours, stopped at a hotel for the evening. After eating and then exercising Bodie, they got him settled in the back of the car.

They both turned in and tried unsuccessfully to sleep. They had far too many unanswered questions and thoughts on their minds.

The hours dragged by uncomfortably, though they managed to get a minimal amount of sleep. Ray let Bodie out and gave him a drink and some food before their breakfast, then they were away, driving again back to where it all started, to the place where Ray started to realise who he was and what he had to do with his life. It was what he had been born for and what he would die for, if needed. This was the path he had to follow, he had no choice now.

Ray drove steadily and was soon turning up the road and heading for the place where his fight really began. He glanced to his left and out across to the woods as the memories came flooding back.

He spun the car around and swung in through the pillars and into the courtyard. He stopped at the centre and looked at the place where the house used to stand.

Chris had been told all about this place and knew what had happened here. She could instantly sense the evil here.

Ray got out of the car and let Bodie out. The dog looked at Ray questioningly, then headed off to explore and mark.

Chris got out and came around, looking out down towards the lake and beyond. Ray kicked the dead earth under his feet; the soil was dry and lifeless, nothing had grown here, and it was just not natural or right.

He walked to where the house had stood. There was nothing left now, nothing that would indicate that a house ever existed here. However, anyone would know something was not right with this place; that there was something abnormal and unnatural here, the atmosphere was unnerving.

Chris turned in a circle, trying to imagine what Ray had told her. The battle Ray had here with the dogs and the creatures from the lake. The whole nightmare.

"Some places are better off dead. I don't think this place ever really lived," Ray said, turning to face Chris.

"It is a very strange place. I can feel many horrid things here. They've been here before you came here, long before the house was here even." She winced slightly and felt her stomach rumble.

"You still hungry?" Ray asked as he heard the sound.

"I'm okay. Are you all right being here?"

"Of course. I fought my battle here and won; this is my triumph, my victory," he said as he watched Bodie sniffing around the two pillars of the entrance.

"Come on, let's look at what we came to see." Ray walked towards the area where the barns used to be.

They noticed the crack in the earth instantly and walked towards it. The circle of stones were still there and the hole looked no more menacing now than at any other, but they knew it had held something evil and powerful for a long time.

They both knelt down on one knee and examined what lay there. Ray peered into the hole, then stood and went to his car. He retrieved a powerful torch from the boot and returned, shining this into the hole. It was only about seven feet deep, lined with solid stone throughout and hexagonal in shape. It seemed to be bottomless; nothing inside except an empty void of darkness.

Chris was looking at the stone for some sort of inscription. She peered in, seeing nothing written on the walls. She looked at the stone, running her fingers across the forged edges. A confused look appeared on her face.

"What is it? What are you thinking?" Ray asked her.

"These seemed to be melted together, like they were forged in a fire or some sort of tremendous heat. What heat can melt stone and forge it together like this? It must have been something extremely powerful back then."

"If Kaden did do this, why have you never found out about it? You said you researched him intensely."

"I did, but there are many black areas in his life that no one seems to know anything about. Where he came from, for one. No one seems to know where he actually came from, he just seemed to get this reputation of killing witches and destroying evil.

Then there was his time before he met Angelique, another black time. There was more recorded while he was on his quest to destroy these things." She looked at him and saw the thoughtful look on his face.

"What if he didn't destroy this thing because he couldn't destroy it? Maybe he had to keep it alive, just confined, for some reason?"

"I don't understand you." Chris shook her head in confusion.

"What is to say Kaden was always good, or came from good? What if this is his alter ego, his dark side?"

"Like some sort of inner fiend that he had to keep hidden? A part of himself that, if it dies, he dies, but this has survived and now wants the other half of itself, the Kaden half?" Chris said.

"Evil never dies, that is why it is still here although Kaden is gone," Ray replied.

"But it sees you as Kaden, so it wants to kill you and revenge itself."

"So, in fact, I am fighting myself, the evil dark half of myself?"

"That is why it can stop the energy of us using the cards and board; that is why it is so fucking powerful." Chris sighed. If this was right and they were, in fact, fighting Kaden, she knew it would be almost impossible to win.

The odds against them were too great, especially in this day and age. It could not be an all out battle. Ray would have to kill to survive and he could not do that in this modern age. He was in the wrong century to fight this thing.

"I know what you're thinking, Chris," Ray said to her. He had watched her expressions and he was thinking the same thing.

"We need help, Ray, but there is no one to help us."

"I need a time machine to go back and take it on its own ground, that's what I need."

"The black arts might be able to help, but there's no way you will get a black witch to do you any favours," Chris said sarcastically.

"I need to find out how it was cast into this hole and sealed. Someone must know."

"Kaden will know, he probably did it. But you can't get in touch with him." Chris shook her head in frustration.

"He told me he is always watching me and always will. If that is so, he should know what is happening, surely."

"He communicated through your Ouija and that is now a closed porthole, isn't it, unless we can get it back open."

Chris wrapped her arms around her belly and breathed out in a little discomfort.

"You all right? Something not agreed with you?" Ray asked with concern, seeing her actions.

"I'm fine, just a little indigestion, I think."

He stood up and looked around the deserted place. He saw Bodie down by the water's edge, looking out into the lake.

Chris stood also and looked down at what Ray was staring at. They both walked down to investigate why the dog was acting a little strange. It didn't take them long to reach the large animal, who looked up at them as they approached.

Ray looked out across the lake and remembered the time he threw the Ouija board out into the water. It all looked calm and innocent now, unperturbed and tranquil. A far cry from when he last saw it.

CHAPTER 6

Chris looked out across the water and frowned. She shivered and wrapped her arms around herself for warmth and rubbed her arms.

"You feel it as well then, do you?" Ray asked without taking his gaze away from the water.

"It's like I have been here before. There is something very strange about this place."

"Bodie can feel it, you and I can feel it, something or someone is here and I think this is where the answer is. I just don't know how to unlock it," Ray said, sighing. He kneeled to stroke his dog.

"Well, in a way it started here for you, so I suppose it would be a good place to finish it."

"It's where to start, that is the problem. The fucking thing could be anywhere. Do I have to wait for it to come for me or do I launch an attack?" Ray shook his head.

The more he thought about the situation the more it was against him. This was no ordinary enemy, not that any of his enemies were ordinary. This time he was fighting his own inner self, his own dark half, the evil that never dies.

"It has killed this place. Nothing lives here anymore," Chris said.

Bodie stiffened and his ears pricked up. He growled and looked at the water. Ray stared at the same spot and he could see a ripple coming from the middle of the lake and moving outwards. It was like a vibration on the water, but pinpointed.

Ray stood and so did Bodie. Chris noticed it and unfolded her arms. She felt the adrenaline rush and her stomach turned. She ignored it and concentrated on the water.

All three were watching this strange movement on the lake. The water seemed to be dipping, sinking in a specific spot, leaving a void.

Ray looked around and started to back up slowly; he wanted more room to manoeuvre if anything was going to happen. Bodie stood solidly and growled louder. His hackles were up and he was ready and waiting.

Ray reached down into his boot and slid a commando knife out slowly. He held this in his right hand and switched on; he was ready, like a coiled spring.

Chris backed up, also searching around. She gave Ray room but also made her own killing ground.

"Go get the car, Chris," Ray said.

The water was vibrating, becoming more and more agitated.

Chris backed up, breaking into a run. She suddenly stopped and turned as heard the deafening roar of something being ejecting out of the water. The water sprayed up, revealing that had emerged.

It was a giant of a man, dressed in an old combat uniform of black, thick, worn leather. The scarred and twisted face bore down on Ray.

The warrior looked awesome and powerful, taking Ray by surprise. He backed off and Bodie sprang at the figure, though he backhanded by the thing and knocked to the ground awkwardly.

Ray ran forward and hit the giant in the stomach with all his force, bouncing off uselessly. He was nowhere near powerful enough to even touch this man. Lunging again, this time with his commando knife, Ray stuck it in deep into the leg of his adversary, just before he was violently knocked back and reeled off by a crushing blow to his head.

Chris dashed to the car and opened the boot; she knew what she was looking for and searched with speed and anxiety.

Bodie was kicked viciously in the ribs as he tried to get back to his feet and was sent rolling back, yelping.

This man looked unstoppable and kept coming, the water dripping of his body. He was from another time but, no matter where or when he was from, Ray was having trouble handling him.

Taking a handful of dry dirt, Ray threw it at the man's face, hoping to gain a few seconds. It had no effect at all. There was no blink, no flinch, nothing; this monster of a man just kept coming. Ray had never run from a fight in his life but the thought danced through his mind now.

The knife stuck out of the giant's bleeding bleeding, though it seemed to have no effect. Ray stood quickly and dodged the right-handed blow aimed for his head.

He side-stepped and brought his foot down hard on the side of the knee of his attacker, again having no effect. He elbowed him in the temple at the same time, which knocked its head to the side momentarily.

Spinning around, he caught Ray in a vice-like grip and pulled him viciously into his head, butting him with a nasty cracking sound. Ray's nose burst and blood splattered across his face.

He was dazed, but his reaction was instinctive and he jabbed his fingers into the eyes of this unstoppable man. He was dropped to the ground and used the precious moments to recover as best he could. Rolling to the side, he was on his feet again moments later, just in time to see the crossbow bolt embed in the giant's chest, reeling him back in surprise and pain.

Chris quickly reloaded and took aim a second time, hitting him in the ribs this time, burying it in so deeply that only a few inches of arrow was showing.

Ray rolled over to the staggering giant and pulled his knife from the leg wound. Bringing his hand across his chest, he lashed out and slit the throat of the giant who was flailing blindly.

The blade did its job well and the jugular was severed. Blood pumped out as the giant dropped to his knees, trying to roar but only managing a gurgling sound as the blood poured down its throat. Spitting deep red blood, it dropped face first into the dirt. The ground was soaked with the thick fluid pumping from the wound in its throat.

Ray looked over to Bodie who was still on the ground, then he turned and saw that Chris had reloaded the bow and was carefully walking towards him, all the while continuing to aim at the giant laying on the ground. She was taking no chances.

Staggering over to his dog, Ray knelt down and touched the unmoving animal. He looked back at the dead giant, face down in the dirt, and gave it a look of absolute abhorrence and sheer hate; if he could kill it again he would.

He stroked the dog's head and it stirred, its tongue hanging out of its mouth. As he came around, he tried to stand, but Ray stopped him, making sure that his friend was not damaged.

Chris stood over the giant with the crossbow still aimed at the head, trying to figure out where it had come from. She pulled her stomach muscles in as the pain gripped her. Fighting the discomfort, she focused on the problem at hand.

Bodie was stood unsteadily. He seemed fine, he had just been knocked out by the powerful blow he had received. He shook himself and walked over to the giant on the ground, sniffing at it. He then cocked his leg and urinated on it. He tried to stretch, but stopped as a pain shot through his side. He was limping slightly, but was okay.

Ray was wiping the blood from his face and nose with the back of his hand, it had splattered over his tee shirt and he looked a mess. He walked over to Chris, put his arm around her and kissed her forehead, leaving a stain of blood from his nose on her hair, which he didn't tell her.

"You saved my life, Angel," he told her.

"You are out of practice, slow, and your timing is off," she said, pulling back and lowering the crossbow for the first time, finally convinced that the giant was dead.

"Don't I know it. Fuck, he hit hard, whoever he is."

"He looks like he is from the time of Kaden in the way he is dressed. Some sort of warrior, killer, assassin maybe?" Chris sighed and looked over at Bodie who seemed none the worse for wear at the moment.

"So what does this tell us? Was he possessed or just summoned, or what?" Ray was confused and his head was still ringing with the battering he'd taken. He took deep breaths of air and kept looking down at the lake, half expecting that something else would pounce from it at any time and come for him.

"I would say it was summoned or brought back. This is not going to be easy, Ray, not at all." Chris backed off and released the bow string on the crossbow, disarming it.

"Have we finished here? I think we should go," Ray insisted.

Chris agreed and they all got into the car. Chris drove while Ray got a towel from the back and cleaned his face off. Bodie laid on the back seat silently, nursing his wounds.

"You're going to have a nice black eye there tomorrow," Chris said, trying to inject some humour without success.

"My whole face will be fucked up, temporarily ugly," Ray said, blowing his nose into the towel and filling it with blood. He wiped the blood from his hands and face and put the towel down in the foot well.

"So where do we go from here?" Chris asked, turning down the lane and out into the main road.

"Away from the population. I cannot afford to have confrontation without protection. If I get arrested, then I am a sitting duck in a police cell and it's all over. I think we should go up north, it's the country I know and it has wide open spaces."

"We have to be careful, this thing could come at us through anybody or anything, I expect, and if giants like that last fucker are being summoned, fuck knows what we are going to come up against. It looked like something from the sixteenth century, which is when Kaden was alive," Chris informed him knowledgably.

"How do you know that? How do you know when it came from?"

"I have seen that battle dress before. I have researched this stuff, don't forget, and I know a lot more about you than you do." She changed gear and sped up as she came to an open bit of road.

"Well there is no one to help us this time, we are on our own, so if you have any ideas, feel free to share them."

"I am just as much in the dark as you, I have no fucking idea what is going on," she snapped at him viciously.

"What's with this outburst?" He asked. It was as if he were talking to someone completely different and not the woman he had lived with and fought side by side with for the last two years.

She shook her head and looked out of the windscreen intently. Ray could sense the upset but there was something else, something he did not understand.

"Tell me what's on your mind and let's get it sorted, because if we are not together, then we cannot go on together," he told her, looking at her blankly for an answer.

Chris looked in the rearview mirror and pulled the car, stopping and turning the engine off. Spinning in her seat, she faced Ray who was looking straight into her eyes, waiting for her to speak.

"I don't know what is wrong, but something is very wrong. We need that bond, Ray, that togetherness, and I am having these feelings I do not want to have about you." She shook her head and he could see she was struggling to understand and explain herself to him.

"What feelings? Just spit it out and stop fucking about." Ray had already lost patience, this was not his strong point and if something had to be said, he wanted it said.

"Don't you speak to me like that!" She was defensive and her tone of voice was verging on attack.

"Tell me what is on your mind, Chris, and tell me now," he insisted, refusing to break his stare.

"I will fucking tell you because I want to, not because you are telling me to." She was very defensive and Ray was put on his guard instantly. "If what is coming for us is you, then will you be able to destroy it? Will you be able to handle it? Are you up for the job?" She looked confused at herself for a moment, shaking her head.

"And is this you speaking, Chris?" Ray watched her very carefully for any sign. The fact that any one of them could be possessed was deep in his mind at this moment.

"Of course it's me. I am just concerned you are out of shape and you are going to blame me for it."

"Don't talk so fucking stupid!" he shouted at her.

"Don't fucking swear at me or I will knock you out!" she shouted back at him, frowning.

Ray looked deep into her eyes. He really needed this woman and he knew it, even if he never told her. She was the strongest woman he had ever come across and she had been through so much because of him.

"Just take a swipe and let's get the anger and the doubt out of you, shall we? You won't make me look any worse."

There was a momentary standoff while they both looked at each other, then a slight crack appeared in Chris's tight lips and she had to smile. The anger and frustration was subsiding rapidly.

"Bastard," she said, and smiled again at him.

"Yeah, I know, but would you have me any other way?" He winked and dropped the side of his mouth into a little cheeky smile, looking at her with his intense blue eyes.

"Well, without blood and bruises and possible broken nose, yeah I would." She grinned back at him and the tension was gone.

He leaned forward and kissed her on the lips.

"You're sexy when you get angry, do you know that? It brings out the Viking in me," he softly said.

"Oh shut up and let's get on with it." She turned back into her seat and looked out of the window as a thought just came to her.

"What is it?" Ray said looking at her

"Viking? Norse. In Norse mythology there are Valkyrie, female beings who are said to carry away the souls of warriors slain in battle. The name derives from Valr, battlefield corpse, and kajasu, to choose. They fly over battlefields and bring back warriors to enter Valhalla, the warrior's paradise," Chris informed him.

"So what has that to do with anything?" Ray asked, confused as usual until it was explained to him.

"What if this thing is something like that. Your dark side bringing back the warriors you have killed in battle, like that fucking giant back there. It was dressed in sixteenth century battle attire, you might have killed that before and it has been summoned back for another shot." She looked at him, convinced that she was right.

"So all the fuckers I have killed in battle are coming back for a second chance at the title?" He sounded discouraged.

She nodded a yes and bit her thumbnail, still turning the idea around in her head. Every bit of information she could get helped her to understand what they were up against and possibly understand a way of defeating it or destroying it.

"It might fit, don't you think?"

"That could be hundreds. Why couldn't he just have been a blacksmith or something, for fuck sake." Ray sat back in his seat and shrugged his shoulders, sighing.

Chris looked at him and, even in this time of trouble and danger, she had to smile at him. He was like a fish out of water in this world and society but sometimes he was like a child and she loved him for it.

"All the information we can get will be a help, and we need all the help we can get, love," she informed him.

They both look up as a police car rounded the corner and raced past with its lights flashing. They watched it disappear into the distance.

"Late for his dinner, no doubt," Ray said, looking at the road ahead where the car had gone.

"Tell me a joke, Ray, make me fucking smile, for Christ's sake."

"Lad comes home from school and says to his day, I had my first sex at school today. His dad says, sit down here, son, and tell me about it. The boy replies, I can't, my arse still hurts, dad."

Chris rolled her eyes and shook her head, thinking how hopeless he was. She started the car up and drove away, heading north up to the county of Yorkshire; Ray's home ground and a place he knew like the back of his hand. If they were to have any chance, it would be there and Chris was determined to fight this with her man. They were a unit and she should never have doubted it. The thoughts she had earlier didn't seem to be hers, but dismissed them, totally committed and loyal to her man, just as he was to her.

As they drove, Ray seemed deep in thought and was quiet. Chris left him to his own thoughts and didn't bother him.

"I think Diane knows something," he said finally.

"What do you mean?" Chris asked without taking her gaze from the road. She didn't like the woman and had no interest in her, but if he was right she wanted to know.

"Well I know she is a broken, bitter woman, but there seemed to me not to be enough reaction there, if you know what I mean. It was as if she knew something or was told something."

"Well you know the trollop better than I do, what do you think?" Chris said, glancing over for a moment.

"I wonder if she talked with Amber while she was possessed and was told something or found something out?"

"She stayed out of the way until it was over," Chris added, considering the possibility.

"She was bitter and twisted, had a lot of hate in her. I wonder if she knows something. Mind you, the bitch won't tell me if she did." Ray was ready to dismiss it.

"She will fucking tell me, I will make her." Chris said vehemently.

"Tommy, the little queer, knows nowt, I am sure of that. Amber is too weak and vulnerable. It has to be their cow of a mother, if anyone." He looked over at Chris, who was turning it around in her head. The possibility was niggling at her.

"It was just a thought. I am at a loss at the moment. There seems to be nowhere to turn," Ray said dejectedly.

"Let's go and confront the slag and see what she knows if anything. Let's go now and then, if we find something out, fair enough. If not, at least we will be sure. We cannot leave it unanswered now that you have brought it up." Chris depressed the accelerator and raced on faster. She now knew where she was going and headed there at top speed.

CHAPTER 7

Ray was on Chris's phone later that day talking to Tommy. He told him to take his sister out for an hour. He had to talk to his mother alone and he would explain later. Tommy was too afraid of Ray not to do it. So, when they arrived back at the house, they knew there would only be Diane there waiting.

Chris pulled up outside and jumped out straight away, marching up to the front door before Ray got his seat belt off.

He got out of the car and called her back. "Hold on, let's just calm down here for a moment."

But Chris was already in kick-ass mode and was banging on the front door before just walking straight in.

Ray followed. He looked back and saw Bodie looking at him from the back seat; he knew his dog had to be let out so he stopped and used this as an excuse to give Chris a few moments alone with Diane.

He let Bodie out and looked around the place. Bodie was glad of the stretch and walk; he marked his spot and looked up as another dog from the neighbourhood was watching him from across the street. The large, shabby-looking dog thought twice as Bodie straightened and looked at it, waiting for it to make its move. It barked a few times to save face but backed off and went away around the back of a house, still barking.

Ray watched and smiled. He patted Bodie and then looked up at the house, where he could hear raised voices.

"Come on, lad, let's go into the war zone and see what is going on. This place stinks and we don't want to be here any longer than we have to." He slowly walked up the garden and Bodie followed.

He stopped as he heard both women shouting, Chris's deep voice louder and harsher. Bodie sat down and cocked his head to one side at the voices coming from the house.

Ray looked at him and nodded. He would give them a few more moments and then go in, he thought. Let them sort out their differences and then get down to the real reason they were here.

No one else seemed to be bothered by the raised voices and arguments; it was the norm on this street.

"If you fucking know something, you stupid fat bitch, you are going to tell me, and that is not a threat, it is a fucking promise." Chris was fired up and stood facing Diane, ready for a fight, not bothered by the fact that Diane was much bigger and looked stronger. She was no match for this little powerhouse of aggression called Chris.

"Who the fuck do you think you are, coming in to my house and shouting fucking threats at me, you little slut?" Diane was staring straight at Chris who was not going to back down. She was determined that this was one fight she had to win.

"Listen to me. I will talk slowly and won't use long words so a stupid dumb ass like you will understand. If Amber said something to you, I want to know what it is now, do you understand, love?" Chris said slowly and sarcastically.

"I will smash your stupid little face through your head in a minute, bitch. Do you hear me?" Diane shouted into Chris's face, which didn't faze her in the least.

"Your breath stinks, do you know that? Just like your house, just like your fucking life, you sad old twisted cow."

"You're asking for it and you will bloody well get in a minute. Where is Ray, where is he?" Diane looked at the door. She took her gaze from Chris because she was becoming a little unnerved at the indomitable look on Chris's face and her strong determination.

"He is being wise and giving us this precious time together, Diane, so we can sort out our differences. You are so fucking stupid you did not realise what you had in that man. You let him go and now you are bitter because you know he has seen you for what you really are. You will never get him back, or anyone else like him, because you are too ugly inside and out."

Diane spun back around and took a swing at Chris's head, but Chris was much too fast and ducked out of the way. Standing ready, she taunted Diane with her smile.

This infuriated Diane and she launched a vicious attack, running forward, grunting and swinging as she did. Chris again sidestepped and caught her with a right cross square in her face, then she grabbed her hair to pull her back and hit her again.

The fight started and it was Diane's weight and size that gave Chris the problem, not her ability to defend herself.

Fists and feet were flying, hair was being pulled out and blood was spilling from noses as the two women fought it out in the front room. A table was knocked over, the television set went flying and they were rolling on the floor, scratching at and hitting each other with all their might. Both were screaming and swearing at each other as they did.

Chris fought well and made her punches count while Diane was just fighting to stay level. She was losing and knew it; her desperate attempts became frantic and she just dropped on Chris with her superior weight to try and stop her from hitting her.

The blood was running down her face. She was hurting from the blows Chris had delivered and delivered well with power and accuracy. Diane had swung a lot and kicked a lot but hadn't hit her intended target; Chris was just too fast and more experienced.

With a pinch and a push, Chris dug her knuckles into Diane's ribs, causing her to twist off her and scream out in pain. Chris rolled away and onto her feet in a fighting stance.

Diane rolled on the floor and finally got up, though not with the grace or efficiency Chris had. She lumbered her weight up onto her knees then dragged herself up using the arm of the pushed back settee.

Chris could not resist this and went forward with a series of punches and then a front kick, reeling Diane back onto the floor again with blood spilling from her nose and lip. She was beaten and Chris was satisfied that she was the victor. She smiled to herself and took a deep breath of air, regretting it instantly; the stink of smoke and stale food hit her throat and made her gag in disgust.

She looked over and saw Ray and Bodie standing in the door, watching her.

"Had fun, have we?" Ray asked her.

"Fucking loads," Chris said, spitting some blood from her lip onto the carpet.

"Did you find out anything?" Ray calmly asked, seeing Diane struggling to get to her knees.

"Just about to ask again, love, won't be a moment." Chris turned and walked to Diane, fists clenched and ready to carry on with this if needed.

Ray came forward and put his hand on Chris's shoulder to stop her. He looked down at Diane struggling to get to her feet. He should have helped her, but he could not find it in him to do so. He watched as the blood soaked face of this woman he once was involved with looked up at him pitifully. She slumped onto the settee, unable to get to her feet, and let out an exhausted sigh and grunt.

"If you know anything, you might as well tell us," Ray said calmly as he held onto Chris, who he could feel wanting to go again for another round.

"You will tell us or we are going again," Chris added loudly.

Diane sniffed and, through the tears, she looked down at the floor and wiped her face as the blood streamed down her face from her busted nose and cut lip.

"When Amber was ill, she told me that you have to come here. You have to visit it by your own choice, that way it will have somewhere to hide, like you've invited it in."

She looked confused and sniffed again, spitting the blood from her mouth out onto the floor. House-proud as ever, Chris thought to herself.

"Tommy asked us to come here, did you tell him?" Ray said.

"No. I knew what he was doing, I gave birth to the little shit. I know him and can read him like a book. He can't keep anything from me, he thinks he does, but he can't." She sniffed and wiped her face again.

"Anything else, did it say anything else?"

"No. I could not bear to see her like that. It said she would be released if you came and there was nothing else, that is all I know." Her head was bowed and she was a beaten woman, sad, bitter and beaten.

"If you had told us that in the first place, things would have been much easier," Ray said, watching as Chris wiped the blood from her nose.

"What are you going to do?" Diane asked without looking at them she just stared down at the floor looking dejected.

"Kill the fucking thing. You won't see us again and we won't bother you again, but if anything comes to you, get Tommy to ring, is that clear? No fucking about, just do it and tell no one anything about us or what has happened. Do you understand?" Ray told her forcefully.

She nodded and bowed her head, crying into her hands. Chris looked at Ray, her clothes and face blood-stained her clothes, and he held back a smile as he led Chris out the door.

Chris sat in the passenger seat and took the towel to clean herself up a little. Ray let Bodie in and got into the driver's side, driving away without looking back.

"You're going to look worse than me," he said to Chris.

"It was worth it. Fuck, I needed that." She blew her nose and filled the towel with blood.

He looked at her, grinning mischievously. "You really surprised her. A little bitty thing like you, she probably thought she'd steamroll right over you."

Chris rolled her eyes. "Just call me the mouse that roared."

Ray chuckled as he drove. He left the filthy estate far behind, though they were both still thinking about what Diane had said.

"You all right? Do you want to stop somewhere to get cleaned up properly?" Ray asked, glancing over at his woman.

"I am fine. We can both clean up when we stop." She shook her head with disgust. "Fuck, that place stunk. My clothes smell of fags and shit and God knows what.

How can someone live like that?"

"Miss a chance in life and feel sorry for yourself instead of moving on and getting on with it," he replied, shrugging.

"So what did you make of what she said, that we had to go there by our own choice?" Chris looked at Ray.

"And it will have somewhere to hide?" Ray looked confused.

"Why would it say that to her?"

"How do we know it is not dormant in me, or you, or even Bodie for that matter?" Ray said with a hint of dread.

"Why not just kill you, if that is the case?"

"It needs somewhere to hide, she said."

"Well, if it needs somewhere, we have to discover where it is."

"We have to visit it by our own choice?" Ray repeated what Chris had said.

"Why should that be relevant? If it knows who you are, why should you have to go to it? Why can't it come to you?"

"Invitation. We have invited it by visiting it." Ray was thinking aloud more than indulging in the conversation.

Chris sat quietly. She had just had a notion and was rolling it over in her head.

They drove into the night, stopping at a place that Ray used to use when he was by himself during his quest years. He had camped here many times and knew it was quiet and easy to defend; the place sat above the river and was very desolate.

He pulled his car around and parked under the large rock overhang, which provided a perfect shelter. The river was only fifty yards down from this and it was on the bend, totally private from surrounding areas.

He put up the tent while Chris went to the river with some fresh clothes and washed. The tent was up, the stove was on, and Bodie was fed and watered by the time she returned, her blood stained clothes all wrapped up in a bundle She put the clothes in the bag in the boot ready to be washed at the first opportunity.

They sat together and ate, not saying much, each lost in their own thoughts. Ray knew something was on Chris's mind, he could see the signs and knew it was best to leave it until she was ready to tell him.

They settled in for the night. Ray had a look around the area just before they did to make sure they were alone and secure. Bodie was left on guard outside as they both crawled into the tent and laid down.

The small lantern lit the inside of the tent adequately enough and they had a sleeping bag each, both cuddled up and facing each other.

"You are going to have a nice black eye there tomorrow," Ray said, looking at the battered side of Chris's face.

"You already have one, so we will match," she said with a little smile that didn't last more than a few seconds.

"You going to tell me yet?"

"Tell you what?" Chris said with a little frown.

"What is on your mind. You're turning some thoughts about and spinning your wheels mentally. What is it?" Ray asked calmly.

"What are you, some sort of mind reader in your spare time?"

"No, but I have known you long enough to know when something is bothering you, lass."

"To be honest, I don't know how to, or even if I *can* tell you."

"Well, you have no choice now, do you, after saying that?"

"It is the thing I didn't want to happen. It must have been when I was on those antibiotics for that infection I had last month."

"What are you talking about?"

"Antibiotics can make the pill ineffective." She studied Ray intensely at this moment for his reaction, but there was none. Nothing, not even a flicker of emotion.

"Are you sure?" he said after a slight pause.

"As sure as I can be. I will have to get a test when we get to the next town; find a chemist and find out."

"Is that the pain you have been having in your guts?"

"Probably yes. Tell me what you are thinking, honestly."

"We have a big problem." He was stone faced serious.

Chris closed her eyes. This was the last thing they needed at this time and it had come and hit her full frontal without any mercy.

"So what do we do?" she asked finally, keeping her stare at Ray's still face.

"Do you remember when that fucker came out of the water at me, back at the farm house?"

"Yes. What about it?" Chris was a little confused.

"You got stomach cramps. I saw but didn't react."

"Get to your point, what is on your mind?"

"It needs somewhere to hide and we have to offer it some sort of concealment, go there by our own choice. It does not invade us because we invited it." He looked at her and saw she was getting the idea.

She shook her head and didn't want to believe it. She felt her stomach turn at the thought.

"No, there must be another explanation." Chris went into denial as a defence mechanism.

"Well, if you can come up with one, I am willing to listen."

"It is not inside me, Ray. It is not inside the baby either."

"I think it is and I think that is where it has been all along. That is why we had to go there and see the child possessed, to give it access so to speak. And that is why, when you get stomach cramps, it seems to be a signal that something is about to happen." His face had not changed expression and Chris felt a little uncomfortable with it.

She rolled onto her back and looked up at the canvas tent above her. She thought about it and didn't want to accept it, though her logical mind came through and she looked at it from a different perspective.

Ray left her with her thoughts for a moment. He knew when to give her space and time and this was such a moment. He crawled out of the sleeping bag and quietly left the tent.

CHAPTER 8

The night had closed in and the moon was almost full, lighting the surrounding area well. Bodie and Ray sat looking out across the river and to the barren land beyond.

Only moments had passed when Bodie growled, instantly putting Ray on his guard. Bodie stood and his hackles lifted; he sensed it but could not decide where it was coming from.

"Ray, Ray, quick." Chris sounded as if she were in agony.

Ray dashed over and peered in. He saw Chris holding her stomach and rolled up in pain, fighting it. She turned to him, her eyes full of hate, though not directed at him. She grabbed her stomach as the gripping vice-like cramp tore through her.

Ray spun around when he heard Bodie growling and barking. He looked up and he could see above him, on the protruding rock, two men. They were small but had stabbing, vicious eyes that directed at Ray. Again, they were dressed in worn black leather, a battle dress of centuries ago.

They did not look white, nor black, some mixed breed, Ray thought. Both held two curved swords each and were poised and ready to pounce. They didn't take their eyes off of Ray, who was staring back at them while trying to decide whether to dash for the car and his armoury. He silenced his dog with one word; he didn't want Bodie dashing into a swordsman, he would not have much of a chance.

It was a standoff for the moment. Chris rolled out of the sleeping bag and up onto her knees, fighting the pain in order to see the events unfolding outside of the tent. She peeked through the vent at the front then, moving away quietly, she pulled the other side of the tent up and slipped out under it unnoticed.

Ray had only a knife on him. He had always kept it on his person in the old days and it something he had started doing again. He reached down and took the commando knife from its place, taped to his lower leg. At least he was armed.

He stood tall and proud, showing no fear. He moved into that space in his mind; the killing ground. Keeping an watchful eye of the two men watching him, he weighed the situation and was ready. Bodie was in position and ready to pounce at his master's command.

Both men bobbed down slightly and moved their heads to one side, looking at Ray as if to recognise him or make sure of their target. Ray could feel the tension rise; he knew it would soon begin and it did.

Both men jumped from the rock together. Ray took aim and threw his knife, hitting his target perfectly in the neck. It reeled back in mid-air, screeching and holding the gaping wound in his neck as he awkwardly hit the rocks.

"Bodie, finish it," was Ray's command, and the dog wasted no time in pouncing on the man and, without mercy, ripping him to shreds, finishing the job within seconds.

Ray was dodging the swing of the sword at this point, as the small but very fast and very strong attacker wielded the weapon with expertise and confidence at Ray's head. Rolling out of the way, Ray frantically looked for an equaliser to fight off this man. He was no match unarmed against a sword.

The only thing he had time to pick up was the small frying pad from the stove which he swung, catching and blocking the blade as it bore down on him. Deflecting it, he moved fast and threw a punch at the attacker, missing and backing off as the sword was swung again.

Ray was focused and managed to deflect the blade once more. The metal of the stainless steel pan crashing against the superior metal of the sword was minor, but it was enough to block it from slicing him in two.

The man stood back and took up a samurai stance, holding the sword in two hands with the blade pointing straight up in front of him. He snarled at Ray, who looked him in the eye, waiting for his next move. Slowly the swordsman moved around, trying to circle his target. Ray, however, knew what he was doing and spun where he stood, always facing his attacker. Bodie came close and growled at the swordsman but was ignored.

Ray kept searching with his peripheral vision to find a better weapon, though he could see nothing within easy reach. He noticed the grip tighten on the sword and came to attention as the attacker again came forward with a series of slices and thrusts. His blade was fast and accurate, but Ray was faster and managed to move out of the way time and time again.

He needed help and it finally came to him in the shape of Chris. She had sneaked to the car and opened the boot. Her cramps were too painful for her to load the crossbow, instead she grabbed two knives and moved quickly towards Ray.

She shouted as she ran, getting the attention of the swordsman. He glanced over and saw Chris throw the knife at him. Moving with great skill, he swung his sword and deflected the knife. He looked pleased with himself, but his glory was very short lived. Bodie pounced and bit into the arm holding the sword, dragging it down.

Ray was on him instantly. He pounded the man across the head with the pan and repeated this several times, knocking the man out cold. Bodie shook his head from side to side and tore a chunk of flesh from the man's arm.

Chris ran over with the second knife in her hand. She lifted it and stabbed it down into the throat of the unconscious swordsman, ensuring that he would not move again. He gasped as the blood oozed from his throat wound and he was dead moments later.

Ray stood and looked across at the first man that Bodie had dealt with. He was still; dead, like his comrade. He put his arm around Chris and held her close.

"Are you all right?" he asked, concerned.

"I will live," she said, looking up at him with dread in her eyes. They stared at each other for moment. The silence was awkward and Ray broke with his brutal Yorkshire honesty.

"There is no doubt now that they are warning signs. How are your cramps now?"

"Weakening," Chris replied emotionlessly.

"We have a problem, Chris, and we have to figure a way to sort it out, or get it out."

"You want to abort the child?" she asked him coldly.

"No, I don't think that is the answer. If you are right, it will just shift to something or someone else. We have to use what we know to our advantage. At least we know where it is and we have some sort of signal if anything is about to happen." He was not too sure about what he was saying and wanted Chris's logic to help with the explanation. It was not coming, however, she just stared at him silently.

She looked around at the two dead men on the ground, she looked at Bodie, who was looking at her and then, turning back, she looked up at Ray and finally spoke in a calm voice.

"You better get rid of the bodies and we better get out of here, don't you think?"

"Talk to me woman, don't just go silent and funny. The problem is there and we have to handle it, not shun away from it or let it fuck us up."

"Well what the hell do you want me to say? Our child is possessed by a demon and it is residing inside me here?" She grabbed her stomach and stared at him with blood-shot, tear-filled eyes. Turning away, she shook her head and ran her hands through her long blonde hair.

Ray said nothing. He walked over and picked up the dead warrior and walked away with him around the side of the protruding rock face. He reappeared minutes later and flung the body over his shoulder, turning to face Chris.

"Pack the tent up and get our stuff together, we're leaving." With that he was gone again around the edge of the rock.

Chris angrily did as she was asked, cursing under her breath as she did. She pulled the tent down and packed the stuff away, glancing over at Bodie. He was watching her from a few yards away, silently staring at her.

She felt the stab of pain in her guts and bent double, gasping. As she shook, she noticed the large dog stand and look at her intently. She began to back up slowly towards the car, waving her hands behind her as she felt her way blindly, refusing to take her eyes away from Bodie.

He slowly edged forward as she moved back. A deep, low growl came from the depths of the large animal as he kept coming and Chris winced as the cramps gripped her. She staggered and slipped over a raised stone almost losing her footing, barely managing to regain her balance just in time. The stabbing pains tore through her and she fell to the ground curled into herself, holding her stomach tightly. Looking up, she saw Bodie moving in and thought she was about to be tore to pieces by Ray's dog. She growled and spat out in anger as Bodie, teeth bared, descended on her.

He stopped suddenly and sniffed her belly. Snarling, he remained motionless as he sniffed the helpless Chris, rolling in pain on the ground.

"Bodie, no!" Ray shouted as he ran over. He dropped to one knee and Chris reached out and took his hand, squeezing it tight as she yelled out in pain.

Bodie backed off and laid down, still staring at Chris, his ears pricked up and emitting a low growl.

Ray quickly looked around to see if there was going to be an attack.

Chris gripped his hand and screamed at him.

"Fuck, Chris, what do you want me to do?" Ray searched around, looking for any sign of someone or something coming for him. He glanced at Bodie, who was just focused on Chris.

Holding Chris's hand, he felt her go limp and pass out. She dropped and was flat on her back, looking peaceful and quiet. Ray stood and again searched around, still thinking it a signal. Bodie cautiously walked to Chris and sniffed her lower abdomen, looking curious and confused.

Ray quickly gathered their things and piled them into the car. He ordered his dog in and then picked Chris up in his arms and sat her in the front seat, easing it back slightly and making her as secure and comfortable as he could before belting her in.

Driving away, he headed for a hospital.

***

Darius Foster was locking his back door for the night and turning out the light. He stopped as a shadow moved and a figure came into sight from behind the wall in his shop.

"I was wondering when you would show yourself," he said, not surprised or concerned at the intruder in his midst.

"You are no match for me and you know it. I am Xander," The large man said in a low growl.

He was dressed in an ankle-length black coat that hid his entire body. He was a powerful man, you could tell that even through the shape of the coat. His face was chiselled and almost gaunt-looking, his eyes black, deep and piercing.

He walked slowly up to the motionless Foster and faced him, towering over the wizard. Foster did not look up with his head but lifted his eyes to look into the face of this menacing man.

"I know who you are. What do you want and why are you here?"

"A shifter has been released," he said with a hint of urgency.

"Deal with it then. It is one of your vile creatures, it has nothing to do with me or my clan."

"Your comrade with the beast must do it. It is he who owns the shifter." He took a deep breath and sighed, looking out across the shop then back at Foster again.

Foster's eyes widened and he felt a bolt of fear coursing through his spine. He lifted his head and looked at the man, not wanting to believe.

"Kaden's dark side?"

"The time is not right for it to be released. It must be brought back under control and sealed until the darkness time is here and then it and the others will be ready to take their place among us." He spoke urgently, though Foster could see the pride in the man, as if he were looking forward to the inevitable as he saw it. Of course he is, Foster thought. The arrogant bastard always thought he would win, though he surprised him with his appearance here.

"You need Kaden?"

"He needs us. He cannot control it."

"He won't trust you." Foster shook his head in doubt.

"This is why I am here. He might trust you, or his woman will and he trusts her."

"I have no trust in you, nor do I want to have anything to do with you or your evil. I am not in the habit of helping your kind." Foster was no match for this powerful black wizard and he knew it, but he was holding his ground well.

"You don't have to trust or even like me, it is not important at this time. Get in touch with Kaden's whore and tell her."

"If she agrees, what is your plan?"

"It must be trapped, which we can do, then Kaden has to entomb it again. It won't be easy, it has an army at its disposal and can call on it at any time, and the whore of Kaden is harbouring the shifter."

"You are scared. You know this is as dangerous to you as it is to anyone else and you cannot get rid of it without your enemy's help. How ironic." Foster favored him with a sarcastic smile.

"Don't anger me, little man, or I will rip your insides out where you stand. This shifter must be captured, it cannot carry on any longer. I will be dealing with the bastard Kaden in my own time; he has taken too many from me and he will pay for it, but this is a more urgent a matter to be dealt with."

"You know they will not help you, they will not agree to anything you say."

"If this shifter kills them, then there will be no one to seal it again and we all will be at its mercy. It is too dangerous and powerful to be left roaming this planet, it must be dealt with!" His voice was beseeching and his manner became impatient. He stood closer to Foster and looked at him more intensely than before.

"I will see what I can do. I cannot promise anything."

"Just do what has to be done."

CHAPTER 9

Ray was drove steadily, trying not to give in to the panic that was threatening to consume him. Not that he would ever admit to it. Concentrating on the road, he didn't notice Chris open her eyes and slowly look around. She took a gasp of air and moaned as she tried to lift herself up from her reclined position.

"What happened?" she asked.

Ray looked at her and then back at the road saying, "You passed out. I am taking you to a hospital."

"Don't be stupid. Get me somewhere where I can get cleaned up."

"You need medical help, Chris, you passed out with pain."

"We both look like we have been in a bloody war, Ray. If you take me to a hospital, they will ask too many questions, draw to much attention to us. Look at your face, look at mine." She moved the wheel on the side of the seat and sat up straight again.

"What do you feel like now, is the pain still there?"

"No, it's gone. It's just a dull ache now." She took a deep breath and looked back at Bodie asleep on the back seat.

"This cannot go on. If it is making you pass out, it is just too precarious."

"Oh, stop trying to use long words, Ray. Too fucking dangerous, you mean." She ran her fingers through her hair and sighed.

"Don't talk to me like that."

"Well it's not you with it inside you, is it?" Chris was suffering from a maelstrom of emotions and realized too late that she was taking it out on Ray.

"No, it isn't, but still don't talk to me like that."

There was an uneasy silence for several moments. Ray did not look in her direction and she did not look in his. They glanced at each other at the same time, then away again.

"all right but you must understand…" Chris said, cut short when Ray interrupted her.

"I understand we have a major problem and I understand you are in mortal danger. One way or another, we have to get that thing out of you and, one way or another, I have to kill it or contain it. That's what I understand."

"One way or another? What is the other way, Ray?"

"I don't mean abort it. I have told you that, so stop having a go at me about it."

"I just don't think you comprehend what the hell I am feeling, what the fuck is going through my head."

"And I don't think you comprehend what the fuck I am feeling either. It is my child as much as yours, it is my hurt and my problem as much as yours."

He slammed on the brakes and brought the car to a sudden stop. Bodie was thrown off the back seat while Chris grabbed the dash board, feeling the seat belt grip and lock as she was thrown forward.

Spinning in his seat, Ray turned to her. His face was stormy and his eyes wide; she had not seen him like this before.

"Calm down, Ray. We need our rationality and we need to be together throughout this, remember?" Chris said before he had a chance to speak.

"Exactly. So what the fuck is all this about? Because divided we fall, united we stand."

"I don't know. It just comes over me, as if it is not me speaking sometimes."
Chris looked unconsciously down at her stomach, then back at Ray.

Piercing the tension, Chris's mobile phone rang and she answered it. Ray watched
as she nodded and said nothing for a few moments.

She then looked across at Ray and asked, "How far are we away from Darius
Foster's place?"

"An hour, maybe a little longer. Why?"

"We will be there in about an hour." She put the phone back into her pocket and
looked at Ray, who was waiting for an answer.

"Be where in an hour? Who was that?" Ray asked impatiently.

"It was Darius Foster, the white wizard we know."

"Yes I do remember the man."

"He says we have to visit him; he might have an idea how to get rid of the
darkness shifter."

"How the fuck did he know about it? What is going on? How do you know it was
really him on the phone?" Ray was instantly on his guard.

"It was him. I think we should go and listen to what he has to say. He is a good
man and just might be the help we need. I don't know why the hell I didn't get in touch
with him before." She shook her head in disbelief at her own shortcomings.

He said no more, he simply turned and headed off down the road. He knew the
roads in this part of the country very well and knew the fastest way to get to most places.
He stopped once to fill the car full of petrol and was soon on the way again, taking a total

of seventy minutes to reach the shop where Darius lived.

Dawn had broken and a new day was brightening the horizon. Parking the car, they all got out. Bodie stretched and shook himself, cocking his leg instantly on the wall by the shop.

Ray looked around, instinctively checking the area, as Chris walked to the door and knocked twice.

A few moments later the door opened and there stood a worried looking Darius. He hugged Chris and put his hand out to Ray, who shook it. They all went in without saying a word.

Darius stood in the middle of the room, about to speak. Bodie and Ray stood while Chris sat down.

"What I am about to tell you, you will dismiss instantly. I then want you to rationally think about it."

"How did you know?" Ray asked him curiously.

"I was told by the dark wizard, Xander."

Ray stood straighter and grunted angrily, his fists clenched as he stared at Darius.

"I know what you're thinking, Ray."

"No, you don't, or you would not be standing there right now."

"Hold on just a moment, please let's all stay friends," Chris said, trying to inject some calm into the boiling situation.

"Fucking hold on? He is in contact with Xander, the blackest, evilest fucker that ever walked this earth," Ray shouted.

"Ray, please calm yourself. I am here to help you, not fight you, and you need much help, my friend."

"I have been hunting him for years and have never been able to find him, and you just say you have had a conversation with him? Where is he now?" Ray looked around, instantly on guard.

Bodie felt his master's tense state and was put on alert.

Darius looked at Chris for support. She stood up and stood between them both.

"Hold on, now, let's just calm down. United we stand, Ray." She looked at him and he looked back at her, saying nothing.

"Shall we sit down and talk about it" Darius asked.

"I defend myself better standing, thanks." Ray was still defensive but was willing to listen, though for how long he didn't know.

"Xander came to see me. I was shocked that such a prominent figure would leave his lair to come here."

"Just get on with it." Ray's patience was diminishing fast.

"He knew about the darkness shifter and told me about it. He knew that you had to contain it, Ray, and he knew it was being harboured by you, Chris, my dear." He looked at Chris with concern in his eyes.

"How did he know all this Darius?" Chris asked him.

"Because he is an evil bastard and knows every fucking thing," Ray said, adding his intellectual contribution to the conversation.

"Well, yes, you're right. He knows all evil, all darkness, the entire underworld." Darius looked back at Ray. He was struggling and knew Ray would not go for this in any way shape or form.

"So why has he come to you?" Chris asked.

"He understands the shifter must not be allowed to exist. It must be contained, especially this one. It is Kaden's darkness and it is all powerful. It must be stopped, and *now*," he emphasised his last word.

"He is worried that something is just as powerful as he is, that something can destroy him. Well, maybe we should let it do the job and save me the trouble later on." Ray sounded irritated but, more than that, he sounded fanatical.

"Calm down, Ray. We have to listen and sort this out. If this man is as powerful and as important to the black arts as you say, then obviously this is beyond dangerous, it is beyond just us," Chris told him.

"No, you listen. I am going to take my dog for a walk and I will return when I have figured out whose fucking side we are all on." With that, he left with Bodie.

Darius started after him, but Chris pulled his arm and stopped him.

"Leave him, Darius, he will be all right. He will mull it over, ask the questions he has to ask himself, and then he'll be back. Don't worry."

Chris and Darius sat and calmly talked over what had to be said; the plans, the risks, the possible outcome. What Xander had said and what Ray must do. It did not sound good and it was a risk that was too much to take, but there was no other choice, they both knew that. There was no one else on the earth powerful enough to trap the shifter and then give Ray a chance to seal it back in the ground.

They talked for a long time, until Chris went upstairs and got a much needed hot bath. She felt much better for it. Darius made her a full breakfast when she came back down the stairs in a fresh set of clothes from the car, while her old clothes were in the washer.

They talked more over breakfast, trying to make some sort of plans, though there was nothing else to do. They just were not powerful enough nor did they have the knowledge to fight the thing. They needed the help of the evil Xander.

***

Ray sat on a park bench, looking out across a small lake. Bodie was away to his rear, smelling through some leaves and marking his spot as usual. The park was quiet at this time in the morning, just what Ray wanted. A few people were walking their dogs and a few of them came up to Bodie but decided against it when he looked at them with a stare that sent them running back to where they had came from.

Soon Bodie came and sat next to Ray, who put his hand down and stroked his loyal best friend. He stayed there for some time, alone with his thoughts and his dread at the realisation that he might have to be in alliance with his arch enemy.

He looked down at Bodie and smiled at the faithful friend he'd had for all these years, the same dog who had saved his life on more than one occasion. The same one that had gotten him out of many a bad situation, the same one that would stick by his side no matter what, the one that would give his life to save Ray's. Never had anybody had such a wonderful companion.

Then Chris flashed into his mind. The woman who came into his life and turned it around, the woman he had fallen for and the one he felt so strongly about. The one who fought by his side and the one who had saved his life. It made him feel lucky to have these two companions in his life.

He stood, then went down on one knee and hugged his dog tight. Bodie licked his face and enjoyed the affection his master was showing him.

"You should have that dog on a lead, young man," a voice came from behind him.

"I will give you one piece of advice and I suggest you take it. Fuck off," Ray said, slowly turning to look at the gentleman staring distastefully at him and Bodie.

"Well, I have never been so insulted or spoke to in such a manner before," he said, screwing his face up angrily

"Get out more. Now, piss off."

Ray stood and looked down at the arrogant gentleman. He huffed and walked away, mumbling something to himself as he scuttled off up the small incline.

"Come on, lad, let's go get some food," Ray said to Bodie. They headed back to the shop and to Chris and Darius.

They walked back into the house and to the front room. Chris looked up and then stood up from her chair, holding something in her hand. Ray noticed they were pain killers.

"What you have there? What are they for?"

"Paramol and ibuprofen, to help with the cramps," she said.

"Are you in pain now?"

"No, I am fine at the moment. I have had a bath and got cleaned up, why don't you do the same?"

"I'm all right. We want food and drink."

"Ray, this is me you're talking to," Chris told him.

Ray walked forward and took her in his arms, hugging her close as he gently kissed her forehead.

"We will have food and drink, then we will talk. Where is the bearded wonder?"

"If you mean Darius, he is giving us a little time to sort things out and see what we can do. He is nearby."

"I'm going to feed Bodie. Is there anything here to eat?"

"I will fix you something if you take a shower. You will feel a lot better for it."

"I'm all right, don't worry about me." With that, he left and went to the car to get Bodie some food.

CHAPTER 10

After both of them had eaten and calmed down, they all sat in the living room again. This time the atmosphere was not as volatile.

Ray sat next to Chris, who had spun in her seat to face him. He looked at her and waited for her to start.

"You're not going to like it, Ray. I don't like it, but unless we can come up with something better, we are stuck with it."

"We can never trust Xander, never."

"I know, but what other choice do we have? He says they have the power to trap the shifter but they cannot kill it or control it, you have to do that. He says he will be able to get it from me and they will circle it get it out in the open, if you like, then we have to go and finish it." She could not make it sound plausible to Ray so she didn't try, she just said it as it was, hoping he would come up with something better.

"They circle it, want me to enter this circle and do the deed, then they will just let me walk away, will they?" He seemed calm and collected, which surprised Chris a little.

"Well, obviously, we have to have an escape route."

"Come in here, Darius," Ray said, without taking his eyes from Chris. Instantly Darius walked in from the other room where he had been listening. "The fact is Xander is scared. He must be, he would not have shown himself if he wasn't. I would not trust him as far as I could piss in the wind; he is worried and needs our help."

"He has the power to control this thing, Ray, something we cannot do," Darius said, sitting across from him in a chair.

Ray smiled and shook his head slightly, letting out a little sigh. Looking down at Bodie, he said, "They have a lot to learn, mate, don't they?" Looking back up, he spoke to Chris and Darius in turn, "He needs us more than we need him. He has to do what we say, there is no other way for him to go. If he doesn't comply, this shifter could destroy us and him and he knows it. He helps us on our terms, we do not help him on his."

Darius smiled and looked at Chris, who was grinning at Ray. It was so obvious they both missed it.

"We couldn't see the wood for the trees," Darius said.

"How is he getting in touch with you?" Ray asked Darius.

"He said he would be in touch. Who knows how this creature will work."

Chris looked around the room and a thought came to her. "He might already be here, listening to our every word."

"Well, it will save us telling him then, won't it?" Ray said, looking at Chris.

"So what is the plan? What shall I tell him when he returns?" Darius asked Ray.

"We need the thing out of Chris and we need it contained or trapped somewhere, then we need to know how to seal it back into the ground or wherever it has to be entombed."

"We need to contact Angel and Kaden, they will know how to do it," Chris said to no one in particular.

Bodie bolted up from his prone position and growled; he looked confused and his ears were pricked up. Ray instantly drew his knife from his boot and stood on guard, while Chris stood beside him.

Darius looked confused and scared for a moment, then slowly stood and looked at

Ray. "I think he is here. What shall we do?"

"My instinct tells me to kill the fucker, but we need to see what he as to offer and bring this to an end," Ray said through gritted teeth.

"Be careful, my friends. He is powerful and terrifyingly dangerous, to the point of being the devil himself."

The room became cold and Bodie became agitated. He backed up and stood next to Ray, not liking what he could sense.

"Show yourself, let us see you," Darius said out loud with his head held high.

"Still, Bodie, still," Ray instructed his dog, giving him a reassuring stroke on his head.

They all stood, waiting for something to happen. The silence was deafening and the pressure in the room became more stifling and thick. The cold and damp increased and they began to see their breath as they breathed out.

Chris felt a twinge in her stomach. She ignored it, but a bolt of pain hit her and another followed in succession. She breathed out in discomfort.

"You all right?" Ray asked without looking at her.

"Hope so. Just stay focused, don't worry about me."

The laugh was evil, pure evil, and thick in sound and body. It rumbled through the whole room and became louder and louder until it was on the verge of causing pain in their ears.

They didn't see where he came from, he just seemed to be there at the front door. His presence was menacing and he moved with a gliding motion that swiftly slid him across the room where he stood in front of Ray, only a few feet from him.

They were face to face, these two enemies, close enough to touch. Ray gritted his teeth and stared coldly at the evil presence in front of him. Chris was doing the same through the pain in her belly and Bodie was waiting for the command of his master.

"Kaden and his whore. How fitting this all really is," Xander said in a low ominous voice.

"Let's get this over with. And the next time I see you, I will kill you, make no mistake about that," Ray told him.

"You are so predictable and so stupid, do you know that?"

"Why have I been wiping your bitches out for the past years then, if I am so stupid?"

Xander's calm face changed into a scowl; his eyes narrowed and a hate-filled stare struck Ray full on. He didn't flinch, even though his heart was almost pounding out of his chest.

"Your time is coming, Kaden, and coming sooner than you think. You *and* your whore." He looked at Chris without moving his head, darting his eyes across to gaze at her.

"We need to deal with the matter at hand," Darius said in a very polite voice that did not fit the situation. He was ignored.

"I knew your mother, Angelique. She was a feisty little thing as well very pretty. We have had lots of fun with her. Do you want to speak with her?"

"I speak with my mother whenever I want. You can't intimidate me," Chris held steady and masked her pain well.

"Oh, but do you? Are you sure? I know where she is and I know what she is like.

We have all tasted her, just as we will with you. In time, you will suffer just like him."

He looked back at Ray with deep black eyes and a stare that would have crushed most human beings.

"You are so wrong and so going to pay for it," Chris told him, although his attention had shifted back to Ray.

"You pathetic creatures are so stupid. You have brought me what I wanted and now you stand here threatening me as if you are something special? You are nothing and will be crushed, tore apart from the inside out." His voice was menacing and hateful.

"We have something to discuss and I think we had better do it," Darius said again, and again he was ignored.

"Kaden, your time is limited. Make the most of what you have because you will be going to my place sooner than you think." A broad grin split his face. He looked at Chris and then down at her stomach, his grin disappearing to be replaced with a frown.

Chris felt the rumbling in her guts.

She fell to the floor in immense pain; something felt like it was being ripped from her stomach. Ray moved forward but was caught with a backhand so powerful it lifted him off his feet and threw him back awkwardly to the floor.

Chris rolled over and cried out, clutching her arms around her midsection. Ray stood, gripped the knife hard and came forward, but he was facing an empty space. Xander was gone.

He looked around and over to Darius, who shook his head having no idea what had happened, his concern concentrated on Chris.

Ray knelt down and rolled her over gently. She had tears in her eyes as she looked up at him. She struggled to her feet and pushed him away, making her way up the stairs slowly as she held her belly.

Ray watched her go and then looked at Darius who held his hand up to stop him.

"She needs a moment, Ray."

Ray looked around the room, at a loss as to what to do for a moment. He looked at Bodie who was looking at him, he looked back at Darius and then up at the stairs where Chris had gone.

"I should have killed him there and then while I had the chance." Ray finally said.

"You had no chance. He was here to collect the shifter. He has lied and manipulated us all."

"And we fucking fell for it." Ray wanted to kick himself but held back the urge to fly off the handle. He looked again up the stairs and then began to walk towards them.

"Ray, I think you should give her a little time by herself."

"She might be hurt, need help," Ray insisted, and went to the bottom of the stairs. He paused for a moment, then slowly went up them, knowing in his heart that he had been right all along.

He looked into the bedroom and saw it was empty, then he looked over to the bathroom and noticed the door was closed. He knocked softly, asking, "Chris, you okay?"

"Go away. Leave me alone please, just leave me alone." Her voice was distressed and worried.

"Chris, I want to help you," Ray pleaded, trying the door but finding it locked.

"Help me by going away and letting me sort this out myself."

"What's wrong? Do you need help?" Ray was on the verge of kicking the door down.

"Leave me alone, for fuck sake," she shouted and then he heard her sob.

Backing up, he was about to kick the door off its hinges, stopped by a calm polite voice from behind him.

"Ray, she is a woman and needs to be left alone to deal with that problem. You cannot help her in there, I'm afraid." It was Darius and he was looking at Ray from the top of the stairs.

Ray stopped. Turning, Darius saw the look on his face. This was something Ray had never experienced and thought he would never have to face in his life.

He bowed his head slightly and walked up to and past Darius without looking at him. He went down the stairs into the living room, where he again sat next to his dog and was quiet, thinking his thoughts, alone with his anguish.

It was some time later when he heard the bathroom door open and Chris walk into the bedroom above him. He looked up and, without hesitation, walked up the stairs. He went into the bathroom and noticed it had been cleaned; the toilet roll was empty and the few specks of blood she had missed were the only things that gave it away.

He took a deep breath and went into the bed room.

Chris was laying on her side curled up on the bed facing away from him. He stood at the door, just watching her quietly for a moment, before asking gently, "Chris, are you all right? Can I do anything?"

She was silent and he almost thought that she hadn't heard him until, eventually, she replied quietly, "Not unless you can bring back the dead."

Ray closed his eyes and took a deep breath. He came to the bed and sat on it, putting his hand on her shoulder. The fact that she didn't pull away was a positive sign to him.

"I am so sorry, so very sorry."

"I have lost it Ray, the baby is dead, flushed away. How fucking nice is that," she said, her voice quivering with every word as she spoke.

He rubbed her shoulder and gave it a squeeze, not really knowing how to handle the situation. He left it for a moment before asking her, "Are you all right? Do you need a doctor or a hospital? Anything I can get you?" Ray was trying to say the right thing, though he had no idea what the right thing was.

"No, I don't want anything. The mess is gone, the life is gone, and I have cleaned up the blood. Don't think there is any need for D and C."

Ray looked puzzled; he did not know what that was and didn't want to ask. He felt hurt, he felt lost and inadequate to handle this situation. He never dreamed he would have emotions like this.

"What can I do to help you?" Ray asked.

"Kill the bastard that killed my child," she turned and looked at him, "our child."

She had tears in her eyes and Ray felt compelled to grab her and hug her. He leaned forward and gently kissed her on the forehead, then laid on the bed with her. He curled up behind her and put his arms around her and she snuggled back and curled up into him. He was going to make her feel safe and warm and wanted.

They lay together for some time. Nothing was said, just being together and holding each other was enough.

Darius stood outside the door. He did not enter, instead turning and walking back downstairs, where he found Bodie staring up the stairs. He could tell the dog was wondering what the uneasy feeling in the house was all about.

"Settle down, boy, they may be some time," Darius told him as he walked past and off into the kitchen.

.

CHAPTER 11

The rain hit the window hard, pelting everything outside. Bodie was laying down at the bottom of the stairs, where he had been for over five hours.

Chris lifted her head and blinked her sore eyes. She felt protected with Ray's strong arms round her.

He noticed her move and spoke in a gentle voice, "Can I get you anything?"

"No," is all she said, though not in a sharp way.

"Are you feeling all right? Nothing wrong, is there?"

"Oh fuck, Ray, you just have no idea, do you?" She turned and faced him. Seeing the concern in his eyes made her regret what she had just said.

"No, I am afraid I don't, but I do want to help you. I have no way of knowing what it is like, what you have been through, and never will, but I do want to help you."

She smiled at him. Touching his face with her hand, she stroked his cheek, then leaned forward and gently kissed it.

He did not change expression or react in any way, not that she expected him to.

"I am so lucky and so very glad I have you."

Ray smiled at her, the same smile that she fell in love with all that time ago. His deep blue eyes looking at her filled with love and affection made her feel so much better about herself. Though the hurt would take a long time to subside, she was grateful she had him there to help her with it.

"Would you like a drink of tea or something stronger?"

"Tea would be fine. I think we better go down, don't you, and see what Darius is doing and how we can sort out this mess."

Ray got off the bed and smiled at her as he left the room. He went downstairs and greeted his dog with a happy stroke, then went into the kitchen to make some tea.

Darius was already in there having a sandwich. He looked up with a questioning gaze. Ray answered him before he asked the question.

"She is a bit shaken up, but she will be okay."

"The child, she has lost the child?" he asked, already knowing the answer he was about to receive.

"Yes, she did, Darius. What is D and C?" Ray asked while making the tea.

"They have to do that if the contents of the uterus as not come away properly. They have to take it and scrape…" he stopped and looked at Ray with concern.

Ray held up his hand to reassure him. "No it's fine, I was just wondering. She says she is fine and doesn't need any medical attention. I trust her judgment."

"I would like my friend to look over her. She is a doctor and will be very discreet. I will ring her if Chris wants me to; I think she needs looking at, just in case."

"What does Chris want?" she asked as she walked into the kitchen. She looked drained and sad, but otherwise comfortable. Slumping down on a chair, she looked at Darius for an answer.

"I have a doctor friend who I would like to have come and look at you. She is a very good friend of mine and already knows about you. Chris, please let her look at you. Can I ring her?"

"I am fine, Darius, really. If I don't feel right tomorrow, you can ring her then, but now, no, I am all right." She looked at Ray who was staring at her from the side where he was waiting for the kettle to boil.

"Have you any biscuits, Darius?" he asked, injecting a little humour to break the uneasy atmosphere.

Chris managed a slight smile and Darius looked at them both in turn, shaking his head. He then pointed to the cupboard on the side. Ray wasted no time in getting in there and taking out a packet of chocolate biscuits. He made the brew and sat at the table munching the biscuits and drinking his tea. Chris cupped her mug and sipped it slowly.

Darius found it all a little bizarre. Saying nothing, he finished his sandwich and took a drink of his own hot chocolate before asking, "So what do we do now?" He looked at Ray and then Chris, who looked at each other and back to Darius.

"I don't have any fucking idea," Ray told him before devouring another biscuit.

"It all depends on what Xander is going to do and why he wanted the shifter," Chris said, sipping her tea then blowing on it to cool it slightly.

"Well I do admire your calmness in this matter, I must say," Darius said, confused.

"You can judge a man's character by the decisions he makes under pressure," Ray said with a nod to him.

"Quoting a past prime minister from the Second World War is not helping, Ray."

"Well it helps me. It was a better time for people being loyal and uniting, the country pulling together. That is what is wrong with this country now, no one pulls together anymore, they are all out for themselves and bickering among themselves while the real issues go on unnoticed. We have to pull together and sort out what to do. It is no good arguing or feeling sorry, we have to get the job done and handle the situation then, afterwards, sort out any problems or differences."

Chris nodded and looked at Darius. He could see they had some sort of understanding between them and he stayed out of it. He just let them get on with it and do it their way. They have survived this long doing it like that, so who was he to say any different now.

"Well, I will respect your decision, but I want to help and I think you need all the help you can get right now, don't you? More than ever before, I would say."

"We need to see if we can use the cards and board," Chris said, looking over her mug at Ray.

"Yes, we do. We need to see if they're still being blocked. Hopefully we will find out how to seal this thing back where it came from."

Chris closed her eyes. She was fighting the pain she was feeling, but it was hard for her.

"Please let me call my friend, Chris. She will look you over and maybe give you something," Darius said, seeing her pain.

"Darius you are a great friend and valued ally, but please stop fussing over me."

"It won't do any harm. Better to sort out anything now than have it cause any problems later," Ray said, as rational as ever.

Darius thought he was being to blunt and hard, but Chris nodded faintly, agreeing. Darius went to the phone and pressed in the numbers while Chris stood and walked over to Ray. She kissed him once and then whispered in his ear.

"I am going back to bed to sort myself out. Would you mind giving me that time alone, please?" She didn't wait for an answer, leaving the kitchen slowly and ascending the stairs.

Ray watched her go, saying nothing. He understood what she had to do, he understood she had to sort this out herself and get her head back straight and focused. He was here if she needed him and she knew that.

Darius walked back from the phone minutes later. "She will pop around in about an hour; she has two calls to do first."

"Thank you. We will get out of your hair as soon as Chris is ready to leave." Ray ate another biscuit and then finished his mug of tea in one large gulp.

"You can stay here for as long as it is needed or you want to. I hope she will be all right up there by herself," he said, giving a worried up in the direction of the stairs.

"She is fighting her own battle and I am sure she will win it and come out a stronger person. She just needs that time and space to recover."

"What about you Ray? It was your flesh and blood also."

"I will handle it another way, my way."

He walked past Darius and called Bodie to the door with him. He looked back at Darius and was about to speak but Darius beat him to it.

"You don't have to explain anything, just do what you have to do. My door is always open for you."

With that Ray left and took Bodie out for a long walk. The rain was still falling but nowhere near as heavily. The water hit and bounced off of Ray's face and body. He never noticed, too deep in thought, trying to decide what their next move would be. It was not the best situation he had ever been in but he was sure it would not be the worst.

Bodie strolled along proudly, his head held high. He knew something was very wrong and was ready to help and serve in whatever way was needed.

They walked up to the park and out by the path to the back of the town, then around and back down next to the pond. They got some strange looks, but Ray was in another world at this time and did not bother what others thought of him, not that he ever did. He was far away from this place, deep in thought.

He arrived back just as the doctor was leaving. She was a large woman and she stopped in her tracks as Ray and Bodie walked in. She was startled for a moment, but then smiled and held out her hand.

"It is a pleasure to meet you," she said cautiously as she looked down at Bodie, who was staring at her guardedly.

Ray shook her hand and smiled, asking her bluntly, "Is Chris going to be all right, love?"

"Yes, she is going to be fine physically, no problems at all. The healing is going to have to be psychological now. I have given her a sedative to help her sleep and she should be out until the morning, I should think."

"Thank you for your help, I appreciate it." Ray nodded.

"Oh my help is nothing compared to what you do and have done. I always wondered if I would ever meet a true warrior and now to meet the warrior and beast is just what dreams are made of." She grinned from ear to ear.

Ray looked across at Darius, a little confused by this strange woman in front of him.

"You are looking at a very good white witch, Ray. She knows all about you and what you have done in this life and the previous. She is a fan you could say, or more of a groupie."

"Darius, that was uncalled for!" she said with mock anger.

"Well whatever the situation, thank you again," Ray said.

She nodded with a smile, then looked at Bodie asking, "Can I stroke this fine animal?"

"Yes, he won't hurt you." Ray touched Bodie once on the head and he looked over at this strange woman smiling down at him and lifting her hand to pat his head.

She stroked him, sighing as she touched the soft fur and large head of the dog. She then rubbed and stroked him for a few minutes, her eyes closed in sheer pleasure.

"Thank you, Ray. You are a very special man and we all owe you much. If there is anything I can ever do for you, please do not hesitate to ask me." She smiled again at him and he returned it.

"You're soaked, you should get out of those clothes," Darius said, giving Ray a much needed exit excuse.

He took it without hesitation and walked past them both and up the stairs to the bath room. Bodie followed and waited outside of the door for him.

"Oh, Darius, he is every bit the man I thought he would be. I don't believe I have just touched Kaden and beast."

"Well you have and, again, thank you for all your help."

"Oh, it was a pleasure, sheer pleasure." She left and hurried to her car; the grin on her face almost touched each ear.

Ray ran a bath and came back down when he heard the door close, watching from the stairs as Darius came back into the room.

"Has she gone?" Ray asked.

"Yes. She is a little eccentric, but a very good woman. She has always wanted to meet you. The last time I told her that I had helped you, she never let me rest until I told her every little detail about you. You have an admirer there," he said with a wink.

"Well that is a bloody rarity, I must say."

"Oh, I don't know. In certain circles you are very highly thought of. I think you would be surprised."

Ray went to his car, got some fresh clothes and dog food, then came back in. He fed Bodie and then went for a long soak in the hot bath water. He shaved, dressed and then looked in on a sleeping Chris before he went downstairs.

Darius had cooked for both of them and he gladly ate it before returning to the main room with another mug of tea and the half-finished biscuits he started earlier.

The night had closed in and it was damp and wet outside, the warmth of the house was welcoming to him. The Yorkshire dales were always a favourite to his; he used to come here often when he was younger, drawn to the scenery and the smell of the country air. He felt comfortable here.

***

Walking with Chris and Bodie, he strolled across the difficult but dramatic landscape. Bodie was sniffing his way along, self-assured as usual, and Chris was hurrying forward in front. Ray had to stroll faster to keep up. She was like a small excited girl. She had never seen such features or views before and was taking it all in with an air of excitement.

Dropping down into a gully, they walked past the ruin of one of the many derelict lead mines that littered the place. Back in the 1820's, Ray explained, these old smelting mills were churning out lead from the veins, and this was a busy and prosperous place.

Then they came upon the area that Chris was puzzled about. Nothing grew here, it was like an arid desert. Again, Ray went on explaining that it is the lead in the ground that prevents anything from growing around the place, gives it that barren look.

The dramatic view and scale of the surrounding area gave Chris a permanent grin on her face; she loved this place. Bodie was enjoying the adventure also. He had many new smells to investigate and places to run free and wild.

They sat now in the tranquil surroundings and laid there arm in arm for a while, Chris suggested they walk up the hill in front of them. Ray insisted it was a hush, not a hill.

Whatever it was, she wanted to go up and over it. She decided to leave Ray basking in the sunshine while she and Bodie went on to explore more of the place.

***

The scream was shattering and woke Ray with a sudden start. He looked around, seeing nothing, though he could hear much barking and fierce growling along with Chris's screams.

He stood up and looked around and up to where Chris had gone. He realised that he must have fallen asleep and it took him several moments to get his bearings. He ran up the hush and looked out over the land in front of him as he reached the top.

He caught sight of the circle of witches stabbing long, pole-like sticks into Bodie as he tried to fight them off, but there were just too many of them for him to beat. The poles hurt him badly and he was losing his battle, going down as the hard wooden poles hurt him. Getting jabbed in the side viciously and hit over the back hard over and over, he was in a bad way and could not last long at all. Blood was pouring from his mouth and from the wounds on his side and back.

Ray was running hard and fast, his heart pumping like a jack hammer in his chest. He shouted out at the attackers, but they ignored him and carried on torturing and beating Bodie to the ground.

Chris's screams ripped into his ears from the opposite side. She was being held by each arm and pulled apart by two very big and strong-looking men. Kicking out and shouting, she was trying to hit the attacker in front of her but was out of range. The two men were pulling her arms so hard she felt them pulling from their sockets.

The tall man in front of her side-stepped her kick and grabbed her hard and tight around the neck. His grip tightened so much that Chris's eyes bulged in their sockets and she gagged for breath.

Ray was still running, though he seemed not to be getting any closer. He picked up his pace and charged forward, shouting out as he did, the blood pumped through his veins. The adrenaline gave him strength and determination, but he was not reaching the two most precious things in his life. They both were being taken from him and he could do nothing about it.

A sickening yelp and crush of a spine sent Bodie to the ground, being pulverized to a bloody pulp by the battering of the poles crashing down on to his now lifeless body.

Chris's her head tilted back and her neck split, blood squirting from the tear being inflicted by the powerful hands of her strangler.

Her arms broke free of their sockets and were limp, the ligaments, tendons and arteries torn through. She was dead in a matter of moments.

Ray stopped in shock, his whole body numb. He was helpless and alone. He had lost everything in those brief moments, allowed the two most valuable things in his life be killed and he had done nothing about it.

His scream was heart-wrenching.

CHAPTER 12

The sweat poured off him and he jolted out of his nightmare. He was sitting in the chair where he must have nodded off. He looked around and saw Bodie looking up at him from the floor. Ray slid off the chair onto his knees. Calling the dog to him, he put his arms around the powerful animal and hugged him tight, relieved to see him. Bodie licked his face, enjoying the closeness.

Ray stood and went to the kitchen. Even though it was dark, he still could see his way around. He turned on the tap and took two handfuls of water and splashed these over his face, washing the sweat off and wakening him fully. Bodie followed and took a drink out of a dish of water that Darius had put down for him. Ray dried his face and took a deep breath; he had had nightmares before, but never like that, never so vivid.

He walked to the stairs and quietly went up to check on Chris, who was still sleeping soundly. He came back down and went out to his car. The night air was damp but welcoming, in a way. Bodie took the opportunity to mark a few places before coming back in with Ray, who had taken his Ouija board and tarot cards from his car.

He came back into the room and turned on a small light, which threw just enough light for him to see where it sat on a small side table. He went and made a drink then settled down in front of the light. He took the board from the black bag he carried it in and placed this on the floor. He glanced at Bodie who was sat across from him then, turning back to the Ouija, he began.

***

Chris woke with the sun hitting her face as it shot through the opening in the curtain. She yawned and stretched, turning to see she was alone. She had slept well and her body thanked her for it.

She sniffed and cleared her throat before sitting up and stretching her back. Looking around, she woke herself up and shook as she pulled the covers back and got out of bed. She was a little unsteady at first and had cramp in her stomach and she stopped for a moment to gather herself. Then she went to the door and out to the toilet. Dressed in a long night shirt, she looked about as she went over the landing the bathroom. She saw no one and came back to the top of the stairs and again, yawning before descending them and into the main room.

"You look shell shocked, lass," Ray said as he saw her come off the bottom step.

"Thanks, love you too," she said with a very slight smile.

"Do you want a coffee or anything?" Ray asked standing in front of her. She hugged him and he hugged her back tightly.

"Love a coffee. Where is Darius?" she asked, following Ray into the kitchen.

"He has gone to open his shop. You had a substantial sleep, lass," Ray told her as he put the kettle on to boil.

"What time is it?" Chris asked sitting down, still a little groggy from the sedative the doctor had given her.

"About eleven, I think."

"Your face looks a mess, Ray," she said, looking at the bruising over his eyes and down the side of his face.

"Thanks, I love you too."

"You're welcome." She dropped her face into her hands and took a deep breath letting it out rapidly. She lifted her head and looked around, rubbing her eyes. She finally was back in the land of the living and waited for her coffee.

"How are you feeling now?" Ray asked as he poured the hot water into the cup, making her the coffee she wanted.

"I've been better. Hope I am never worse," she said expressionlessly.

He brought the coffee and stood in front of her, looking at her swollen face. Her bruising was not as bad as his, but it was still apparent, showing she had been in a fight.

Taking a sip of the hot drink, she smiled and relished the taste. Ray always made a good mug of coffee, she thought.

"Do you want to talk? I have something to tell you."

"Is it good news, bad news or fucking devastating news?"

"I can use my Ouija again. I think you should try your cards. I was in contact last night and it is sending us north again."

"You have a fixation with the north, Ray, something always sends you there." She took another sip of her drink, looking at him over the brim of the mug.

"I was born there; Yorkshire born and bred, lass," he said with a hint of pride in his voice.

"Yes, I know, but there is something else, a draw or calling I think, something is there you have to finish."

"Do you feel up to looking at your cards, see if you can find anything else out for me."

"For *us*. Don't think you are leaving me out of this, no fucking way. I want in and I'm going to get the bastard who ripped that life from me." She narrowed her eyes and frowned at him. He was not going to argue with her and she knew it.

"Well, whatever it is, the board is sending us up there. I think you should try your cards."

"We have made a shambles of this, Ray. We have charged in, not understanding what we're dealing with, and have paid the consequences for it. Now we're in a worse mess than ever."

"Out of practice, that's all it is," he tried to reassure her.

"Serious trouble, grave danger, that's what it is, and possibly the beginning of the end."

"Stop thinking like that or I am going alone. Chris, you are no good to me or yourself with negative thoughts like that."

"Practical thoughts, Ray. We have fucked up and it is going to kick us right back in the teeth if we are not careful."

"So what the hell do you think we should do, just sit around and wait for it happen?" His voice became annoyed and agitated.

Chris looked at him for a moment and said nothing, then sniffled and said firmly, "Get me the cards and let's see what we can find out."

Ray went to the car while Chris took some painkillers for the cramps she still had. A short time later, they both settled at the table in the kitchen. Ray spread his Ouija out and gave Chris room to deal her cards.

Chris put her hands on the deck and closed her eyes. She had been away from these for a long time, but now they felt good, better than ever. The force was back and the power was running through them, she could feel it. She began and Ray just watched her.

She looked puzzled and then serious as she kept dealing and laying the cards out in front of her.

Looking up, she took the cards back and then turned them over one by one and said in a calm voice as she did, "I see a child and some hidden darkness; tragedy and fear." She looked up at Ray who was looking at her more than the deck she was dealing. She dealt more cards.

"Fighting and blood and a secret." She stopped when she turned the card she had in her hand. It was the black devil card.

Ray reached forward, touched her hand encouragingly and said in a reassuring voice, "Carry on, don't be afraid. We have each other and will win this like we have won the rest."

"Ray, it is death," she turned the last card she had in her hand, "the lighting struck tower; destruction and great tragedy," she told him, looking at him with worried eyes.

Ray turned to the Ouija. He placed his hands on the planchette and asked the question, "Kaden, I need your help. How do I destroy this thing that has come to harm us?"

He looked at the board but nothing happened. Chris turned in her chair and looked at the board also, then up at Ray, who had become intense looking. The board quivered and a flicker of life moved the planchette. It shook but did not move straight away.

Slowly, Ray felt the power take over and he allowed the pointer to move on its own. It went to the letter S then W and O slowly moved to R then finally D.

"Sword, it has spelt out sword?" Chris said.

"What sword, your sword?" Ray asked.

The pointer moved to YES.

"How the hell do we get a sword from the sixteenth century?" Chris asked, shaking her head.

Ray looked at her and then the board. He was in deep thought and stopped breathing for a few moments then started again. Chris didn't understand and just watched him; she had not really seen him on the board before and never really knew how he worked it, so left him to deal with it as he would.

"Can you place the sword somewhere for me? Can you locate the weapon so I can find it now, here?" Ray asked.

The pointer moved again to NO.

"Where is the sword I must use?" Ray asked unperturbed.

Chris watched as the pointed spelled out its message, then spoke the word out loud. "Xander? He has the sword?" She looked at Ray with dread in her eyes, this was becoming impossible.

"Is the sword in the north? Has Xander hidden the sword? Do I have to find it before I can destroy the shifter he has taken?" Ray asked serenely.

YES. The board shook as the planchette moved over it.

"What does it mean, why is the board moving?" Chris asked.

"Frustration, I think." Ray took a deep breath and asked another question. "Will I know when I see the sword? How will I know it is the right one?"

O-N-L-Y O-N-E was spelled out.

"Where do I look for the sword?" Ray asked quickly.

N-O-R-T-H D-E-E-P H-O-L-E D-A-R-K-N-E-S-S

Ray took his hands off the pointer and turned to Chris who looked a little confused at seeing him looking so satisfied.

"Sorry, Ray, but that was not enough for me," she said, puzzled.

"A few years ago, I was hunting down a witch in the dales; I knew she had gone to ground. I felt such a presence that is was overwhelming, coming from deep down in the earth. I never knew what it was. I think I know now." He looked her in the eye with a cold, calculating look.

"You have been where the sword is?" Chris sat up, suddenly alert to every word her man was going to speak.

"I got the witch and thought that was the end of it. I am sure what I was feeling at the time, although I'm not sure, was the calling of Kaden's sword."

"So, if you can go back to that place, we might be able to get the sword and, if we can do that, kill the shifter?" She frowned as she said it knowing the shifter cannot be killed.

"It came from the ground and I think I have to send back to the ground with the sword of the man who it came from originally."

"I saw death, I saw a child. Kaden and Angelique were tricked using their child, that is how they got Kaden in the end, we know this for sure."

"Our child would not have been developed, Chris," Ray said innocently.

"It was still a life, it was us!" Chris shouted at him.

"It needed a bit of both of us, the baby, to use against us?" Ray said thoughtfully, while he let Chris vent her anger in any way that she needed to.

"Just like Kaden and Angelique, their child was taken and used against them."

She was breathing heavily as the idea began to make sense to her.

"It has what it wants. The question is what is it going to do now that it has what it's got?" Ray asked, leaning back in his chair and stretching out his arms. He arched his back and moaned as he stretched himself.

"Xander has the shifter and the sword and all he has to do now is wait for us to come to him and he will try and kill us."

"He knows we have to go for it, we have no choice. He thinks he is holding all the cards," added Ray.

"From where I am standing, I think he is, Ray."

"False sense of security, it has brought the greatest of men to their knees and made heroes out of ordinary folk. You should never underestimate your enemy. Never." Ray seemed to be almost smiling and it confused Chris somewhat.

"Do you know something I don't? I wish you would share it with me if you do."

"No, not at all. I just know where I am going now and what must be done. I have a target to aim for, a goal to reach. It makes me feel more in control when I know what the hell I am doing."

Chris thought for a moment and the more she did, the more she could see what he meant. They were blind before but now they can see what they must do and where they must go.

"We know our purpose and know where it is, and what it is. All we need to do now is beat it and destroy what ever comes our way." Chris smiled and nodded, finding it odd that she was doing so in these circumstances.

"Exactly. Fight like fuck and show no mercy, lass."

Ray looked a different man, like the old Ray she first met. It had happened instantly and made her wonder for a moment how such a transformation could take place. She had never met anyone like him before and never expected to again, so nothing he did really surprised her anymore.

"So we go north to the Dales?" she asked.

"Fuck knows what will try and hit us on the way and what will come for us when we are there. But yes, that is where we need to be when you are ready."

"I am ready now. Don't worry about me, I am fine and fighting fit, don't ever doubt that," She told him with a stern voice and stare.

"I never doubt you, Chris, and I know you are always there. I trust you lass. No matter what happens, don't you ever doubt that," he said in just as stern voice with the same stare back at her

He stood up and walked to her. She slid off the chair and stood up, facing him. He looked down at her and put his arms around her and she moved into his embrace, feeling safe and warm and loved. She closed her eyes for a moment, relishing the feeling. Snuggling into his broad chest, she put her arms around him and hugged him close. They stayed there for several minutes not saying anything because they didn't have to.

The rest of the day was spent making sure they had what they needed in the car, Ray packed it very carefully, making sure it was all secure. Bodie was exercised and fed, they had dinner and, when Darius returned, they told him what they had found out and discussed it with.

He could not throw any more light on it and Ray was satisfied that he knew what to do and that confidence rubbed off onto Chris.

That night they slept well, no nightmares for either of them. Bodie kept guard downstairs and he could feel the electrified rigidity that had returned to his master. He knew only too well what it meant and was ready, as always, to do whatever it took to achieve what he had to achieve to survive and keep himself and his master safe and alive.

CHAPTER 13

Early next morning they said their goodbyes to Darius. Chris took her phone off the charger and put it in her pocket, double-checking that Darius had her number.

They both knew they were driving into the most dangerous situation they had ever been in. The mood was quiet, though it soon relaxed. It had to, it was just too intense.

"Have you been to the dales before?" Ray asked, as if they were merely out for a Sunday drive.

"No, I can't say I have. I've heard it is a beautiful place."

"Yes, it is, very nice. My favourite place, in fact. When this is all over, I will take you there to explore the great vastness of the Yorkshire countryside."

"You sound like a tour guide."

He continued with his tour guide tone, "It is set in six hundred and eighty miles of national park. We are heading for the old lead mines and the old smelting mills that used to prosper there in the eighteen twenties and thirties. We are going to head up through Skipton and past Bolton Abbey and Grassinton. We have to be careful of walkers and such. It is such a popular place and busy. Even though it is wide open and looks deserted, suddenly you come across walkers and cyclists."

"Could be very awkward," Chris said, nodding her head.

"The old mines are still there, sort of, and the lead veins run deep into the countryside. You come across open holes in the ground and they run through to the other side of the hush and sometimes down into the earth. Over the years they have collapsed and…"

"The other side of a hush?" Chris asked.

"Hill. They're called a hush."

"I didn't know that."

"Fucking hell, I have said something you didn't already." He smiled and she returned it, but there was no feeling in the gesture at all.

"Do you know where we are going exactly? Can you remember where you were when you felt the pull that you talked about?"

"Yes, I know where it is. We will have wide open moorlands and sheltered river valleys."

"You are quite knowledgeable about the area." Chris looked over at him and had a quiet thought to herself.

"I have spent a lot of time there in the past. I used to visit Bolton Abbey when I was a kid. I always loved the place; I felt safe and at home there, for some reason."

Chris took some painkillers from her jacket pocket and flipped two out, swallowing them in one gulp without water. She replaced the rest and sat back in the seat, looking out of the window.

The mood was quietly edgy as they drove. Neither of them knew what to expect when they got there.

"Are we going to have to go through population, Ray?"

"I am going to avoid it as much as possible, but some, yeah. Why, do you need anything?" He glanced over at her.

"No, I'm all right. I just keep looking around and thinking that, at any moment, something could attack us and we have to be ready. If we're on the open road, however, we are more vulnerable and an easier target, don't you think?"

"Before I met you, I used to drive all over the countryside, and I now know some of them knew I was coming. I always thought the same as you, that I had to be aware at all times, never let my guard down. Looking out at every movement and sound; every person was a potential threat. It takes up a lot of your time and energy. I don't let it slip entirely, I don't become complacent, I've just learned not to worry about it. I just handle it when it comes and if it comes I destroy it and move on. If something attacks, we will handle it. No good worrying about if it might or what if it does."

Chris looked across at him and could see he knew what he was talking about. She knew she would never doubt, him never take him for granted, and never leave him.

***

Driving for several hours, the scenery changed to more open and remote views Beautiful, but also dramatic and tranquil, all at the same time. You could lose yourself here and never come back. She could see why Ray liked this place; it was his sort of land, a living landscape, quiet and natural. He was just living here in the wrong century.

"We have to leave the car and walk the last part of the way, are you all right with that?" Ray asked as he slowed and pulled the car to a stop.

"Stop asking if I am all right. I am fine, just a bit of stomach cramp now and again. The pain killers are taking care of it, but I do need a piss," she said, looking at him with a hint of discomfort.

"Hope it comes out all right for you," Ray said, turning off the engine and stretching his back.

They all got out together. Bodie stretched and shook himself, then he went off doing his usual thing. Chris disappeared behind the car to do her thing and Ray just stood and looked at the magnificent views in front of him. He took a deep lung full of country air and smiled at the freshness and cleanliness of it.

He stayed there, lost in his thoughts, until Chris came back around and stood next to him.

She looked out across the wasteland of the moors and scanned the area before saying, "How far do we have to go?"

"About a hours walk, if we're steady. I think we should eat and drink before we set off."

He went to the car and sorted Bodie out with food and water before they both took a drink themselves and ate some cold food they had packed.

The weather was warm but not scorching, the clouds were dispersing in the sky to let a beam of sunlight through, and the day was at its best by now.

It took them a little time to sort out what they would take. Ray armed himself from head to foot with an array of knives and a silver knuckle protector.

"What's with the knuckle duster?" Chris asked him.

"Old friend," Ray said as he slid it into his jacket side pocket. Chris wanted to take the cross bow but sighed as she knew they would not be able to walk through the countryside with it without drawing attention to themselves.

"It's not a lot, Ray, to say what we might be coming up against a few knives and that's it."

"We can't take much else and it doesn't matter what we are taking, it just matters who is behind what we're taking and that is you and me, so have some faith."

She blinked as she processed what he said, then replied, "I have nothing but that in you, I am just being critically cautious, that's all."

"Are you ready?"

"I was born ready," she said, walking past him and up the incline in front of them.

Bodie waited and followed Ray as he strolled off up the same incline a few moments later after looking at his dog but saying nothing. They caught Chris up and they all walked at a nice steady pace over the rough terrain. The views were breathtaking, but Ray's mind was elsewhere at this time.

He went back in his mind, remembering the path he walked the last time he was here. It was a few years ago, though he still remembered it well. It wasn't the first time he had visited the place and it wouldn't be the last, he hoped.

The weather was nice and warm, not too hot. They saw some other walkers in the distance but paid them no notice as they were heading in the opposite direction anyway. Neither of them spoke, they just headed off in the direction Ray indicated and kept going. Bodie ventured off to the side every now and again when he caught sight of something or smelt something that needed investigating and marking.

In other circumstances, it would have been a beautiful walk, a pleasant day out.

Heading down into a gully and then up a steep incline, Ray stopped and looked around to get his bearings. He looked around and down the way they had come, then back up the way they were going.

"You all right? Are we heading in the right direction?" Chris asked him, catching her breath.

"Yes, I am fine and I know where I am. Have you made sure you know, just in case you have to get back to the car for some reason?" He looked at her, his expression serious and stern.

"I will find it, no fear of that," she said convincingly.

Ray nodded and then headed off again, followed by Chris and then Bodie bringing up the rear after sniffing down a hole he had discovered.

It was over an hour later when Ray stopped again. He looked down into the ravine and said, pointing, "There, the old smelting mill, well, what's left of it."

Chris looked at where he was pointing. It was a derelict smelting mill, nothing now but some stone and a pile of old timber. It had been here since the eighteen twenties, collapsing and decaying. A little work had been done on restoration and safety, but otherwise it was just an old wreck of a building.

The tranquillity of the place was comforting, but Ray did not look too comfortable at this time. He was staring down towards the mill, then up past it.

"Is this where you had the encounter with the…" Chris silenced herself after Ray lifted his hand and signalled her to be quiet.

Ray turned to Chris and said in a quiet voice, "There is a steep drop the other side of this hush, then below that the shaft that digs into the earth. There is an opening to it. I think that is where we need to be."

Just then Ray's face changed to a state of disbelief and disgust.

"Hello there, lovely day." A young couple walked past them carrying two large bags. Ray had no idea where they'd come from. Both smiled at Ray and Chris and just strolled past them and down into the gully Ray was about to descend into.

Chris looked at Ray who was looking at her shaking his head.

"What the fuck? And where the hell did they come from?" he asked, looking at the two walking down the hill in front of them.

"I don't know, but I hope they bugger off, because if they…" she stopped as she saw them stop and admire the smelting mill remains, then head off up the side exactly where Ray had pointed they must go.

"I don't fucking believe this," Ray complained.

Chris saw them go to the hush top and then stop. They took something from their bags and both sat down. She looked closely, trying to see what they were doing.

"They are artists," Chris said as she noticed them get their painting equipment out and start to paint the scenery in front of them.

She sat down and sighed. Looking up at Ray, she had to smile to herself. Even in these circumstances, it was quite amusing. Ray did not see the funny side and spat on the ground, rubbing it in with his boot.

"I am going to tell them to fuck off," he said, ready to march down towards them.

"Ray, just sit down and calm yourself. If you do that, they will report you and we do not need the attention. They will go soon and we can carry on. Rest up and let's plan what we are going to do, cover our options."

Ray looked at her and then back at the couple painting in the distance. He walked over and sat down with a grunt and a huff.

Bodie rolled onto his back, stretched his legs up and scratched himself on the ground, moving his body from side to side and making a pleasurable growling sound as he enjoyed the scratch he was giving himself. He stood then shook himself and stretched. He looked over and could see it was a rest time, so he went off exploring and sniffing his way around.

Ray sat looking down at the couple with disgust in his eyes.

Chris took some pain killers from her pocket and swallowed them, Ray looked at her and before he could say anything she said to him, "Yes, I am fine. The pain is easing and the little I have, the tablets are taking care of."

"I was going to say do you fancy a shag, but…" he turned away and looked at Bodie rummaging over some old timber.

Chris smiled and the tension was temporarily lifted.

"Ray, what do you want to do when all this is finished?"

"What do you mean, what do I want to do?" He turned and looked at her, waiting for an answer.

"When we have done this and it is over, what do you want to do, where do you want to be?"

"You're not getting all soppy on me again, are you?"

"No, I am bloody not, I am just asking you a simple question. I could see you found it very hard to settle and I want to know where you really want to be. I don't want to sound like a shrew or anything, but I would like to know." She was serious again and Ray could see she wanted an answer and would persist until she got one.

He moved close to her and looked her straight in the eye.

"I am not very good at this, you know that, but I want to be with you, love, and once this is over, we will go away somewhere and have some time to ourselves; no hunting, no fighting, nothing, just us."

"You found that hard to say, didn't you?"

"Like I said, I am not very good at this sort of thing. Just because I find it difficult to say, though, does not mean I don't mean it." His eyes were melting hers and she had to smile at him, a little smile but a smile all the same.

She laid back and looked up at the sky above her, closed her eyes and took a deep breath. For a few moments, at least, she was going to forget the past traumatic time and relax. The calm before the storm, the peace before the battle, the tranquility before the eruption.

CHAPTER 14

Ray watched as the couple painted their pictures and he became more and more annoyed. It seemed like an eternity, but finally, as the light was going, the couple packed up and headed off.

Ray stood and shook himself. He was ready, Bodie did the same. Chris opened her eyes and sat up then looked down and saw the two people were gone.

Standing, she stretched out and looked at Ray, who was looking down at their target. He was remembering the last time he was here and she left him alone with his thoughts for a moment before saying, "Where do you think it is, underground?"

"Yes, I believe that is where it is."

"So what is your plan? How do we get down in the ground to find it?"

"I have a feeling it will find me. Come on, let's go."

He headed off and Chris looked around. Seeing the light fading made her a little nervous, the night would drop in very soon and they would be in total darkness if there was not a moon out. Looking up, she sighed and then followed.

Heading down past where the couple had been working, they went up the rough country and then down again into a small valley, until Ray stopped and stood still.

"Can you feel that?" he asked, without looking at Chris.

She stopped and tried to feel what he was but could not sense anything at this time. "No, what can you feel?"

She looked at Bodie, who was agitated and growling very low; his hackles were up and he was rigid. She knew they were close, very close and, taking the large knife she had put down her boot, she stood ready.

Ray pulled two slim but sturdy knifes from an inside jacket, holding one in each hand with his eyes narrowed. He seemed to be smelling the air. It had turned cold and the darkness was descending at an alarming rate, visibility worsening by the minute. It was rapidly becoming a very dangerous situation.

Ray slowly walked off to the side, seemingly looking at something. Chris could not see anything except dark landscape in front of her.

Then suddenly she saw it, movement on the floor. A dark shadow, moving ever so slightly, but enough for her eye to catch it. It put her instantly on guard. She gripped her blade tightly and was ready.

"I see it now, there on the floor," she said quietly.

"See them? There are five, at least," Ray told her.

She didn't doubt him even though she couldn't see them.

"Where the fuck they come from?"

"The hole over there, the old mine shaft, I would say." He nodded over to his left.

"I can only see one, where are the others?" Chris was trying desperately to catch sight of the other shadows.

"You go for the one you can see. It has spotted you, so will probably come for you anyway. Bodie will take the one he is looking at now and I will take the others."

Chris concentrated on the black shadow laying low about fifty yards in front of her. She looked closely, seeing the flicker of movement and then could make out the hideous face staring at her.

It was a black witch, the ugliest she had ever seen. Snarling and grinding its teeth at her as it crawled on the ground with animal-like movements.

Bodie jumped and was wrestling with one only a couple of yards away. Chris had no idea it was even there. Bodie's ferocious jaws were ripping into the screaming witch with tremendous power and speed. The witch never stood a chance. Shaking his head, Bodie tossed her aside like a rag doll, blood dripping from his snarling mouth.

At this point, four others were flying towards them, screaming like banshees. Chris swung the knife at the one she had been watching. Bodie sprang like a gazelle at another and brought her down with his weight and power.

The other two flew at Ray, who skilfully swiped and stabbed with his two blades as they descended upon him. He moved constantly from side to side and back again, knowing that it was harder to hit a moving target.

The rips and cuts sliced the oncoming witches to pieces, destroying their offensive. They screamed and dropped to the floor, cut to shreds, unable to even score a single hit on Ray.

He stood on one's head and plunged his blade deep into its throat, cutting the jugular from the inside out. The other witch rolled off and tried to stand, but the blade shot through the air and hit her in the chest, knocking her backwards as the second one he threw embedded in its head, piercing the skull.

Chris had done her job well, shaking the blood from her blade and watching it spatter on the ground. Ray could see the dead witch behind her. He scanned the area, unable to see any more.

"Round one to us," Chris said, coming over to him.

They all walked cautiously down to the hole in the side of the hill. It had been repaired, though it didn't lose its derelict appearance. It was pitch black, the only light they had was moonlight. Well prepared, Ray pulled a strong flash light from his jacket pocket and shined into the hole.

They all reeled back at the sight of the screaming face coming towards them. A huge woman scrambling up and out of the hole fat and smelly and ugly and drooling at the mouth. Chris looked disgusted and reeled back.

The rock was a primitive weapon, but effective, as Ray picked it up and threw it hard into the face of the oncoming monstrosity. He shone his torch and caught sight of the rock hitting her full in the face. He kicked out his boot as she scrambled out of the hole in pain, bleeding and screaming, catching her under the chin and tilting her head back. Wasting no time, he went forward and jabbed her in the eyes with both fingers, mussing the eyeballs back into her head and blinding her instantly. She rolled up and out of the hole holding her face while blood poured through her fingers.

Chris moved forward and stabbed her through the back of the neck. Pulling out the knife, she did it again, and the large witch was silent and still.

"Thought fucking Diane was back there for a moment," Chris said, looking at Ray, who was peering down the hole again with the light.

They could feel a rumble in the ground that came from deep within the earth. Bodie tilted his head to one side and looked down the hole. Chris, momentarily startled, stood ready as Ray peered down the mine shaft. It was too small of a gap for him to stand in. He would have to crawl in, something he was not happy about doing.

The rumbling got louder, and the ground under their feet shook more and more, almost as if something was coming up from the depths of the earth and getting nearer and nearer all the time.

Ray stood back and looked at himself then down at Bodie. He could get down the hole easily. Shining his flashlight back down the darkness of the hole, he saw a reflection of something then a flash of light from within. He peered in, though he could not make out what it was.

Chris looked down and tried to make out what it was, but was just as much at a loss as Ray was. Then Bodie stood and moved to the hole. He seemed in a trance, listening to something that only he could hear. He walked to the opening and leaned forward to look in. He sniffed the edge and let out one bark.

"Bodie, back here," Ray commanded. For the first time ever, Bodie ignored him and continued looking down the hole.

"Hold on, Ray. He is not scared, not aggressive; he can hear something we can't, so leave him," Chris said, looking at the large dog in confusion.

Ray backed up and scanned the area around him. The darkness clouded the whole area and the blanket of black made it all look ominous. He shone the light back down the hole.

Bodie suddenly jumped and was gone down the pit into the darkness, out of sight in an instant.

"Here, Boy," Ray shouted, almost in shock. He fell to his knees and tried to catch him, but he had already gone.

The rumbling was louder and stronger. Ray peered in the blackness and shouted his dog's name but there was nothing, no response at all.

"Fuck it, I am going in after him. You wait here," he said, putting one knife back in his jacket and the other in his mouth. Biting the blade between his teeth, he knelt down, though before Chris could stop him or Ray could go in, Bodie appeared with something in his mouth. It was the sword. He struggled to hold it in his powerful jaws.

Ray backed up. He could see Bodie was being helped out of the hole by a powerful and large hand pushing him from behind. Ray took the large sword from the dog's mouth and put it on the ground by his side, then he reached and pulled his dog free from the hole.

There were two powerful arms and then, suddenly, a bolt of light shot from the dark hole. There in all his glory was Kaden.

Hovering in the air at the mouth of mine shaft, he looked enormous and formidable. He looked down at Ray, who stood and looked back at him.

"You have no time, they are coming. Get safe and do what you must do. May it be well with you," he said in thunderous voice. He glanced at Chris for a brief moment and was gone.

They were both gob smacked. Ray picked up the sword. It was a formidable piece of steel, heavy and impressive. He liked it and held it out in front of him admiring it for a moment.

Chris heard it, Bodie heard it, then Ray heard it; the screams and shrieks bellowing from the pit.

"Time to run, Ray. Come on to the car."

"I've never run in my life," Ray boasted.

"Well you are now. Come on."

Chris headed off up the hill, Ray followed and Bodie came up the rear. They ran hard and fast, dodging the rocks and scanning the ground for ditches and uneven places. Ray looked back and saw them pouring out of the hole. Witch after witch flew up and into the air spun round and then raced after them.

Chris was running fast, but Bodie was faster. He knew exactly where he was going, he could smell his scent strongly. Ray was bringing up the rear. He held the heavy sword in two hands and ran as fast as he could.

They could hear their pursuers racing after them. Ray could feel one very close and just could not resist it, he spun around and swung the sword out, falling short as the witch rose high over him. He spun on his heels and ran into a jump, lifting the sword up. He caught her on the thigh, bringing her down violently and finishing her with a swift slice across the midsection. The large, sharp blade did its job perfectly, nearly cutting her in two.

Ray was impressed. The blade was formidable and he wanted to keep it.

More witches flew from the hole and raced after their intended victims.

Chris was feeling the cramps and breathing heavily while Bodie was well in front and heading forward, leading the way. Ray had caught up by now and ran alongside his woman, glancing back constantly as the noise of the oncoming army of evil became louder.

"You keep going, I am going to slow some down a bit," Ray told Chris.

Chris was in no mood to argue, she just gritted her teeth and ran faster.

Ray slowed and turned. He could see them in the moonlight, speeding towards him. The first one to reach him didn't last long; he beheaded her with great skill and swift action. He surprised even himself; he had never thought of himself as a great swordsman. It was as if someone else was yielding the sword for him and he was grateful for the help, whatever or whoever it was.

The second witch flew for him. Ray sidestepped it and stabbed the blade deep into the stomach of the crying banshee-like creature and pulled it out again. Kicking the witch to the floor, he brought the heavy blade down and severed the head in one slice.

This was one useful and beautiful weapon, he thought. He just caught sight of Chris looking back at the top of the hill, then disappearing over it. He picked up his pace and ran. His lungs began to burn, the sword was heavy and the extra weight was hard to carry.

The following witches were not stopping, they were catching up and slowly closing the gap. Ray struggled and fought through his screaming lungs. Grunting and shouting, he raced faster and faster, making every step count.

The darkness was thick and the night was deep black in front of him. He reached into his pocket and flicked on the flashlight, illuminating his way and making life a little easier. He put the torch in his mouth and rested the sword over his shoulders behind his head, a hand on each end. Running, he went up the hill, fighting all the way.

He stopped at the top to gain a few needed breaths of air. Looking down the hill, he saw them all coming just as quickly up it, not faltering at all.

"Fucking bitches," he muttered before carrying on down the other side and onward. The downhill descent was faster, though not any easier; the jolt on his knees was uncomfortable.

He had no idea how long he had been running, but it seemed liked forever. He was slowing down and had to stop for a moment. He could hear the yells and screams coming up from behind him. He put the sword down and stuck it in the ground, point first. He took deep breaths and stretched his arms out to stretch his back. Taking a big lungful of air, he looked around, trying to get his bearings.

He dropped and bent his knees to stretch them while he had the chance then, taking the sword back across his shoulders like before, he started again running but not as fast as before. His energy was draining and he was tired.

He dropped down onto the path, recognising where he was. He knew the car was not too far, which gave him strength and he picked up his pace.

The witch flew over his head; he heard it, but did not see it. They had caught him up. The second one flanked his left and a third to his right, keeping pace with him; he could see them out of the corner of his eye.

He did not stop, he never even slowed his pace.

A large group were right behind him and another overtook him, screaming at him as they flew overhead and headed off in front of him. He let go of the sword with one hand and held the butt in his right, ready to swing the weapon when necessary. The noise was loud, the shrieking intense, and it made the blood pump through his veins fast and hard.

He could not run anymore, he needed the energy to fight. He stopped and swung the sword in a full circle, which they easily eluded. He took great gulps of air and stood solidly with the sword held in front of him, ready. If he was going to die, he wanted to die on his feet and fighting.

They circled him, about to pounce, when the light shone straight at them. It was the full beam of the Sierra headlights. A growling dog appeared from nowhere and tore into two witches with great speed and ferocity. Ray wasted no time and lunged forward at the one directly in front of him, his sword battering her down to the ground.

The arrows were silent but deadly as they found their targets. Chris stood by the side of the car taking aim with her newfound favourite weapon, the crossbow. She picked her targets well and accurately brought them down.

Ray was swinging and slicing everything in sight. Bodie was fighting like he had never before and the battle was bloody and fierce. Blood splattered everywhere and cries and violent attacks were filling the battlefield they had made for themselves here.

Chris reloaded and took aim once again. She had become very proficient with this weapon and enjoyed the power it gave her. She brought down a screaming witch that was running towards her, then calmly reloaded and fired again at a second one on its way towards her. She stood her ground and stayed focused and in control, something she had learnt over her years with Ray.

Bodie was relentless in his quest; he was ripping and tearing into the witches as they tried to pounce on him. He was just too big and strong for them to get near him. Ray had finished off more of them and his adrenaline rush had given him newfound strength. The sword was covered in blood and guts, but he still swung it with great speed and grace, catching and cutting and killing when he intended to.

The savage battle went on and the carnage was dreadful; bodies and blood everywhere. Suddenly there was silence. Bodie breathing heavily as he came over to Ray, who was gasping for breath as he looked around for another target.

Chris searched the area and could see no more movement. The pile of dead bodies around her man and his dog was a frightening sight to see.

They were silent for a moment, then Ray dropped to his knees, exhausted and in pain. Bodie came to him and smelt at his face then licked it once. He sat next to him and waited for his next command.

Chris ran over and put her hand under Ray's arm. "Come on, we have to get out of here." She pulled him up and they all staggered to the car.

Bodie jumped into the back while Ray stumbled into the passenger seat, still breathless and trying hard to get much needed air into his lungs.

Chris put the crossbow and the sword into the back and slammed the boot. She raced around and got into the driver's seat, then reversed the car over the rough ground. Turning the wheel, she put it into first gear and was away.

CHAPTER 15

"What took you so long?" Chris asked as they drove off down the narrow road.

Ray looked at her. He was unsure if she was serious or trying to be funny, so he ignored the question. He sniffled and looked out the back window, then at Bodie, laying on the back seat, licking his paws and legs.

"I'm knackered, lass, absolutely fucked," he said, winding down the window and taking in deep breaths of night air.

"You were lucky, we were all lucky. A few more minutes and you would have been history."

"You came just in time. Thank you," he said, winding the window back up. His lungs were not burning as much now, and his breathing was not as heavy.

"We are out of shape, out of practice." She winced and Ray could see her stomach had not liked all the running, but he didn't mention it because he knew she didn't want him to notice.

"Damn right, we are. Although you didn't do to bad getting to the bloody car that fast, thank God."

"I used to run in high school back in the good old U S of A. Mind you, it was a long time ago." She glanced over and could see the blood and guts all over him from the battle.

He had calmed somewhat and his breathing had calmed also. He looked out of the window and across the barren landscape in front of them.

Driving fast but not knowing where she was going, Chris kept checking her mirror instinctively and watching the countryside like a hawk.

They drove into the night, away from the battle and the bloody mess they had left behind. Too many questions would be asked if they were spotted, and they had to get cleaned up somewhere; they could not be seen with Ray as messy as he was.

Driving down a narrow road, Chris spotted a river silently running past the embankment. She slowed and pulled to a stop. Ray knew what she was thinking and got out of the car instantly with Bodie following.

Chris went to get some fresh clothes from the back while Ray looked around, checking the area. He removed his blood-soaked clothes and went into the running water, which felt cold and sharp against his naked, aching flesh. It made him gasp and lose his breath for an instant until he became accustomed to the cold.

Chris threw him some soap and he washed the battle remains off his body and cleaned the blood and stains from his flesh. He went under the water and then reappeared, wet hair and soaking flesh. He washed his hair and body while Chris kept guard.

Bodie was in the water, paddling about and enjoying the sensation of the cold water running over his legs and paws. Chris shook her head and thought how the big dog looked so playful and harmless at this time.

Ray walked naked from the river, water dripping from his muscular body. He shook himself and caught the large towel that Chris threw him and she watched as he dried himself and then bent down and rubbed Bodie to dry him as well.

She smiled to herself before walking to the back of the car. She opened the hatch back and looked at the sword. Its shiny metal looked new and unworn. She lifted the heavy metal and held it out in front of her. It had been around since the fifteen century and had seen many battles and fights, but it looked in pristine condition. It was beautifully balanced and honed to a razor sharpness and she lifted it up, lost in wonder for a few moments at the sight of the magnificent and legendary blade.

Ray came around from the front of the car and looked at her admiring the weapon in her hands.

"Beautiful, isn't it?" he asked, looking at the sword.

"Never seen its equal and never will, because there isn't one. Just think, Ray, what this sword has been through and what it as seen. The power it possesses is mind numbing, really." She had so much admiration for it she was lost in her own world for a moment.

Ray looked around as he finished rubbing his hair with the towel. He left her to have her moment while he placed his blood-stained clothes in a bin liner bag and packed it away in the back of the car. He was ready again. Looking around, he saw Bodie was at ease and this put him at ease.

Chris finally came around and placed the sword carefully in the back, covering it so that any prying eyes would not see it in the back of the car. They got back in and were away minutes later.

The full moon looked large and light; the night was crisp and clear. The darkness was beautiful and yet somehow disturbing in its way of covering everything in a blanket of blackness.

"So where and what now?" Chris asked, driving back up the narrow road she had just come down.

Ray placed the knife down his boot and covered it with the bottom of his jeans.

He sat back up, placing the knuckle duster in his side pocket once again. He made himself comfortable in the seat before replying.

"We have the means to contain it, all we need to do now is find it. It is strange but when I was in mid-battle with the sword, I was having flash backs of the farmhouse for just an instant. I don't understand why." He frowned and looked at Chris for an answer.

She glanced over to him and was in thought but said nothing for a moment. Finally, shaking her head slightly, she asked, "Is that where we need to go, do you think?"

"Well it came from there, it was sealed there, and it was if the sword was trying to tell me something, crazy as it sounds." He shook his head at the stupid thing he had just said.

Chris did not think it was stupid at all. She nodded and smiled at him before saying, "You just might have it there, Ray, you just might be right."

Bodie's ears pricked up moments before the scream hit them. It was vile and deep and menacing and full of anger, seeming to shake the whole car from the outside in.

"What the fuck is that?" Chris said, startled.

"Sounds like something is pissed right off," Ray replied, searching around to try to catch sight of whatever it was that was screaming at them.

The large dark shadow flew above them silently, with unsurpassed speed and power, landing fifty yards in front of them. It stood solidly in the road, staring at them with the devil in its eyes. It was Xander, looking more powerful and bigger then ever as he stood in the path of their car.

"Ram the fucker!" Ray shouted at Chris who, without hesitation, depressed the accelerator and pointed the car directly at him.

She braced herself and her knuckles turned white as she gripped the steering wheel. Bodie was laying down; he was experienced enough to know the situation. Ray put his hand out and braced himself against the dashboard.

Xander's eyes were deep black and staring at them intensely. The car raced and the two litre injection engine roared out its power to the back axle driving the wheels. Moments before impact, Xander darted up like a bullet out of a gun and was above them as the car sped past the spot. Chris kept going and could see the horrific figure flying after them with great speed in her rearview mirror.

Ray looked out the back window and saw the face of this vile creature peering in at him. Bodie was growling, frightened. He had never felt such evil or sensed such power before.

Chris didn't know where she was going, she just kept in control of the vehicle and headed down the winding road as best she could. The loud hammering and shaking of the car surprised her, but she kept in control as the large fist pierced the roof of the car and the large powerful hand came straight through.

Bodie stood and snapped at the hand. Ray took the large knife he kept in the glove compartment and stabbed the hand, driving the sharp blade through and out the other side, ripping into the flesh and crushing the bone. He twisted and pulled to the side to slice and do as much damage as he could. The hand was withdrawn quickly and blood dripped from the gaping hole in his car's roof.

He held the knife ready and looked around, seeing nothing until a fist crashed through the side window, shattering glass everywhere and hitting him full in the face. It reeled him back and to the side into Chris, who pushed him off her with her left hand while still driving and steering with her right.

Ray shook his head, dazed but okay. The wind rushed in through the broken window, bringing the noise of the roaring engine into the car. Bodie was growling as Ray watched for any more attacks, while Chris drove, keeping her concentration on the road ahead.

The roar and power of the voice was immense as it shouted, "Kaden! Kaden!" It was the voice of the shifter coming from Xander's mouth.

The arm reached in through the side window and Ray stabbed at it with his knife, frantically trying to slice the intruding grasp of the large hand looking for its grip on something. Blood again splattered over Ray's face and down over the seat and front window as he stabbed at it.

Chris could see lights coming the other way. Another car was heading for them and beyond this was a population. She raced forward and headed for the light, passing the oncoming car at a dangerous speed.

They slowed and steered into the small village. All was deadly quiet and only the odd light was on. She spun the car around and stopped, looking out of her window at the awesome sight in front of her.

Xander stood on the corner, staring straight at them. His hand was red with blood, his face twisted with anger and his soul harbouring the shifter. The combined force glared at them and then was gone, rising up and away into the darkness.

Ray looked at Chris, who looked blankly back at Ray. Both were confused but relieved that Xander had fled. A car turned the corner and drove slowly past them, then was gone again.

They were not sure where they were, but they slowly drove around the streets until they found an open area. It was a deserted car park, giving them a clear view from all sides.

Chris turned the engine off and spun in her seat. "Why did he leave?" she asked Ray.

He leaned back and let Bodie out of the car to explore and do his thing, then turned back and looked Chris in the eye.

"I have no idea, but at least we know where the shifter is now. It makes it a bit easier for us."

"Glad you think so. Nothing like it being easy, eh?" she said sarcastically.

Her mobile phone buzzed in her pocket, so she took it out and answered it. Her face was blank, then a confused look came across it for a moment as she listened to the voice on the other end. She pressed the button and put it back in her pocket, then turned to Ray.

"That was Darius. He is coming here to help."

"What you on about, coming here?"

Just as he said it, a car's headlights shone at them as it turned into the car park and slowly came up to the side. It was Darius and his doctor friend.

"We thought you might need some help," Darius said, winding down the window and looking at Ray and his blood-splattered face. Ray just looked back at them in confusion and then turned to Chris, who looked just as confused but a little relieved that they were here and the number on their side had doubled.

"Your phone, it acts like a beacon. So long as you have a message from me on it, I can track you with my phone and it tells me exactly where you are. Satellite navigation and all that," Darius explained, seeing the confused look on their faces.

Again Ray had to clean blood off of himself. He didn't really believe Darius, but let it go for now. Jan, Darius' doctor friend, gladly helped him. Although he didn't want her help, he put up with it for now.

Chris told Darius what had happened and how they had got the sword. He listened intently and stroked his beard as he did, taking in every word and imagining every action in his mind.

Ray moved back from the car, satisfied that he was clean enough. Jan followed him and they returned to Darius and Chris. Bodie stood on guard and did his early warning system bit while the four of them talked.

"We better get out of here, we might give the impression we're swingers or something." Jan chuckled, not seeming to take the situation as serious as she could do.

No one was impressed or amused, but they agreed with her initial suggestion.

"Okay, look, we appreciate you coming to help, but to be honest, you will be more of a hindrance then a help. So, if it is all the same to you, I would like you both to go home," Ray said as politely as he could to Darius and Jan.

"Listen, Ray, you have a secret army at your disposal and we all want to help you. We may not be warriors but we have skills that will be of great help to you," Jan said, walking up to face him.

"Ray's right, but we would like for you to accept our thanks for all you have done and want to do," Chris said, seeing Ray getting frustrated with this large woman standing in front of him, staring into his eyes.

"We have all been in contact and we believe you have to cast the thing back to where it came from in the first place," Darius said to them, still trying to be helpful.

Ray looked at him with a curious eye, then at Chris, who was already looking at him anyway.

"And what makes you think that?" Ray asked, looking back at Darius and giving him his full attention.

"We have discussed it and just thought it out. It was cast there for a reason, and it must be a reason only Kaden knows. Where else can you take it and seal it except where it came from." He shrugged his shoulders and looked satisfied.

"Xander is here and very near, it is dangerous for you to be around us. I think it is better if you leave and get to safety," Ray insisted to them both as Jan came up and stood next to Darius, while Chris stood next to Ray.

The momentary silence was shattered by the fierce growl and bark of Bodie, he was bolt upright and barking into the distance. He knew it was coming before anyone else could see it or hear it.

"Get out of here now!" Ray shouted, turning to face what was coming their way.

Before any of them could move, Xander was there, ominous and powerful. He was grinning down at them all from his elevated state four foot above the ground. He stared at each in turn and then snarled at Bodie, who continued to growl through his fear.

The voice that boomed out of his mouth was that of the shifter, and it was directed at Chris.

"Would you like to see what the bastard you both made would have looked like?"

It grinned at her as she stared back at it with hate in her eyes.

Darius and Jan held onto each other and shook with fear; they had never been so frightened in their lives.

Tilting his head, Xander looked at Ray and smiled, holding his shredded hand up where Ray's knife had cut it deeply.

"Should have been your fucking throat," Ray said, refusing to drop his eyes from the eyes glaring back at him with hate and vengeance in them.

"You are such pathetic creatures, pathetic little useless vertebrates." The voice was Xander's again, and his glare turned to Chris, who was snarling at him, her stare full of venom.

"Don't hate me because I took your bastard child. You both must know you're doomed and will never have a life worth living. When I take you to my place, you will be forever in…"

Chris shouted, interrupting him, "We have heard it all before. It is you who is on borrowed time. We are going to destroy you and that thing you are harbouring, so save your vile breath, you're going to need it when we have finished with you." She stood strong and was unafraid.

Ray smiled to himself at the guts of his little woman, even though the thing she was talking to was probably the most powerful adversary they have ever come across.

Xander's expression did not change as he spoke in a calm but disturbingly formidable tone, "We shall see. This is the beginning of the end and you just cannot understand it. You are both mine, have been for some time, and I will relish the fact that I will be taking you both to my place sooner than you think." He was confident and spoke down to them in a growling tone that turned it a deep, malevolent hiss at the end of his sentence.

Ray looked Xander in the eye as he walked over to stand next to Chris. Tilting his head, Xander stared at him through black eyes that emanated pure evil. For once, Ray did not say anything, he just looked back at the maliciousl face of Xander and stared into his eyes.

Chris glanced up at Ray, confused by what he was doing. Both these titans just stared at each other. Chris became concerned that Ray was being hypnotised. She clenched her fist and glanced over at Bodie, who was riveted to the spot, but poised to pounce if he was needed. She knew he was there for them. Whether or not Ray was, she was not sure for a few seconds.

It sent her cold for a moment but she heaved a sigh of relief when Ray smiled and said to Xander in a strong voice, "For years I have heard about you, for years I have wanted to kill you, this greatness called Xander, the dark one, the all powerful. Well, you don't seem all that powerful to me. You talk too much. If you want us, we are here. Let's finish it now, one way or another."

Xander's expression did not change for a moment, then his eyes narrowed and his lips tightened while his body vibrated from the inside out. The voice he spoke in was not his, but the shifter's once again.

"You are mine. I will kill you when I want to kill you and not before. I have your child, I have your soul and I have you to command as I wish. I will send my army to destroy you, to cause you pain and agony, loss and suffering. You will pay for the darkness, for the centuries of frustration and misery, the torment and torture of being caught and encased and having my freedom taken from me. I will take you to my place and I will have you to do with you as I wish." The demented smile that appeared Xander's face was horrific.

Ray stood solid as did Chris, both ready for whatever Xander would throw at them.

To their surprise, Xander simply rose up and took a deep breath, before moving backwards and being swallowed by the impenetrable darkness.

CHAPTER 16

Jan was whimpering like a little scared puppy dog and Darius tried to calm her, though he was not in a better state himself.

Chris turned to them and asked the question without thinking, "You two all right?" They nodded, leaning against each other for strength.

Ray walked forward to where Xander had been and looked up and around the area. He was gone. They were alone again and it was quiet.

Chris came to his side and took a deep breath before saying, "Well what was that all about? Why the hell did you go quiet and just stare at him?"

"I wonder who is in control, Xander or the shifter. They don't seem to be working in harmony, do they?"

"You're not making sense and I am not in the mood for games or riddles."

"Neither am I. It is not a game, lass, far from it. He was trying to kill us when he attacked the car. The witches from the mine shaft tried to kill us. He had the opportunity to try here and now, but he didn't. And now he is spouting off that he doesn't want to kill us yet, just make us suffer? I think Xander has taken on something more powerful than he can handle. I think they're a conflicting force and he is having trouble controlling it."

"So what now what the hell do we do now?" Chris looked back around at Jan and Darius then back at Ray.

"We get those two out of here and to safety and then we figure out what we are going to do."

They both walked back to Darius, who was looking at Ray with wide eyes. He swallowed to lubricate his dry throat before speaking, unable to hold back any longer.

"Oh my God, that was terrifying. How the hell do you two stay so calm and in control? I wanted to piss myself."

"You have to get out of here. We will handle it from here. Thank you so much for your support," Chris told him, trying to be kind, but running out of patience nonetheless. The sooner they were gone, the sooner they could finish this.

"You can not drive round in that car, it has a smashed window and a hole in the roof," Jan said, looking at Ray's Sierra.

Ray ignored her and went to his car. He opened the door and began to clean the shattered pieces of glass of his seat and from the floor. He forced the bent sheet metal back up and pushed it back the best he could into the hole where Xander's hand had come through. It did not look right when he had finished but did look a lot better and Ray was satisfied with his quick fix. He took some duct tape from the boot and taped across the hole from inside of the car, forcing the material and interior back into place and did the same on the roof, making in almost waterproof.

Chris insisted Darius and Jan leave. She thanked them again and Ray came and did the same. Finally, they reluctantly but quickly left.

As they drove away Ray asked Chris curiously, "He can not track you by your mobile phone, can he?"

"I am not sure. I think it can be done, but whether he can do it from his phone, I don't know, to be honest. You can be tracked professionally by your phone, I know that."

"Yeah, but Darius is not James Bond nor is he in the Secret Service, is he?" Ray became curious and mistrustful all of a sudden.

"No, he is not. To be honest, I would not be surprised if he doesn't have friends or knows someone who knows someone, if you know what I mean. Their circle is a very large one, even better than the masons."

"Strange, if you ask me, very strange." Ray turned and looked at his car appraisingly. It looked none the worse for wear in the dark, but daylight would be another matter.

Chris looked into the darkness around them. It was silent again; Bodie stood on guard and Ray looked at his car.

"You need to get cleaned up a bit, Ray," she said, looking at the bloodstains on his face. She went to the back of the car and brought back a small towel with a bottle of water. She reached into her pocket and took two painkillers out, swallowed them and then took a little drink of water from the bottle. She then emptied a little water onto the small towel and came up to Ray. She wiped the bloodstains from his face and neck and tried to make him look a little more respectable.

He stood quietly as she cleaned and lovingly saw to her man, savouring the moment and he didn't even complain when she rubbed too hard on his sore nose and face which was still swollen and tender after the fight with the giant.

"Give us a kiss," he said, looking into her eyes.

She did so without hesitation, slowly and sensually, then with a little cheeky smile she winked and took the towel and water back.

Ray looked around, agitated. He did not like it here, it did not feel right to him. The place had no life and he wanted to leave.

"What do we do, Ray, where the hell are we going?" Chris asked, walking back over to him.

"I am not going to just wait around for the fucker to pick us off, I am going back to where we are going to seal it and wait for it to come to me. I am not chasing all over the country looking for it, they always seem to know where we are, so let them come to us. We have the sword and I have the will to use it."

"What we waiting for then, let's get going." Chris walked to the car, stopping just as she was reaching for the driver's door handle.

"I will drive," Ray said as he rushed around to the driver's side and jumped in.

Chris let Bodie in and got in herself, realising why Ray wanted to drive. The side window was no longer there and the breeze streamed in as he drove off. She said nothing but noted it and would repay him when the time was right, she thought. Her hair was blowing everywhere and she was cold from the breeze as he sped on back down to the old farmhouse where it all started for him.

"Do you want me to tape the window up for you?" he asked with a little smirk on his face.

"It's noted, Sibson, and I will repay you in time." She ran her fingers through her hair and moved it from her face, then leaned back to get out of the stream of rushing air and settled back in the seat.

She had become accustomed to how Ray handled things and the way he seemed to have no worries. She knew his mind would be racing with ideas and plans and possibilities. She was quite content to leave him to it and knew he would handle whatever came their way. And she was learning the same attitude: don't bother it until it bothers you. It made her feel better and calmer inside herself. But it did not take away the seriousness of the situation and she knew they had a fight on their hands.

Chris's phone rang. She answered it and listened while glancing over at Ray.

"Darius, we are all safe. Please stop worrying, we will be in touch if we need you." She saw the look of distrust on Ray's face as she was talking to Darius. She grunted a few more times and said a few unimportant words before switching the phone back to stand by.

"Why is he meddling all the time?" Ray asked her, glancing over with a frown.

"Just concerned, I think. He has been in it with us and seen what we have to do, maybe it has shocked him somewhat."

"No, he saw us before when he helped us the last time."

"You don't trust anyone, do you?"

"No. I trust myself and if you can do that, you have all the trust you need." He looked at her and saw the slight twinkle of hurt in her eye.

"I see. You don't trust anyone?" Chris said, looking out of the window and away from him.

"I trust you and I trust my dog, but after you two, no, I trust no one."

"You trust me and your dog?" She spun her head around and glared at him. She was on the defensive and ready to stand her ground here.

Ray looked at her seriously for a moment then back at the road, his face slightly cracking as a smile broke through.

"You are too touchy sometimes. Of course I trust you, woman, you're the only person on this planet I would trust."

"That's better. I was about to swipe you one there." She calmed down and settled back in her seat more contented.

She could see his grin out of the corner of her eye. Smiling herself, she said no more, just thought of what lay ahead.

The night sky was close and the air rushing in smelt fresh. She could not stop herself from glancing about, up and around every now and again. She half expected to be attacked at any moment. Being on guard was not a bad thing, she thought.

They drove most of the night, finally stopping at a small service station to get petrol and stretch their legs. Chris went into the ladies room while Ray walked Bodie on the grass verge.

A tall, big busted woman saw Ray and got out of her sports car where she had been watching him for a few moments. She was leggy and very attractive. The sort of woman any man would die for. Her long, brown hair dropped down her back in a gleaming sheet and the tight leggings she was wearing showed off her sexy figure perfectly. She walked up to Ray and stuck her false but nonetheless magnificent chest out, forcing it against the buttons of her read satin blouse that were struggling to keep it under control.

Bodie stopped sniffing and watched her as she walked towards Ray, who turned and faced her before she reached him.

"Hello there," she said in a low husky voice, smiling.

"Do I know you?" Ray raised an eyebrow as he stared at her, immediately on the defensive.

"Would you like to?" She let her tongue lick her top lip as if it was unintentional.

"Not really. Now, if you don't mind, I am busy."

"Hey, why so rude? I saw you from my car over there and wanted to say hello. Now there is nothing wrong with being friendly, is there?" She grinned and showed her perfect but false smile.

"If your selling, love, I am not interested, now please just go away, okay. I have asked you nicely." Ray was losing patience and it showed in his tone of voice and his body language. Bodie came up to his master's side, sensing that he was unhappy.

"No need to be hostile. I was watching you. I just wanted to get to know you. I saw the drab thing you came in with and I am sure you could do much better than that. A handsome man like yourself and, looking at your face, a fighter as well. I like fighting men. I could give you much better and much more than she ever could."

"I bet you just love to have men fight over you as well, don't you? You could never give me what she gives me, never in a fucking lifetime of lifetimes. That drab thing, as you called her, is worth a hundred of you, love. Do you know why? Because she is a real woman, not a false, spoilt little brat like you. Now take your false tits, your false looks and your horrid personality, if you can call it that, and fuck off, please." Ray looked her straight in the eye, unwilling to back down.

She froze in shock for a moment. No one had ever spoken to her in that way, no man had ever turned her down. She looked nervously back to her car, then noticed Chris looking at her curiously as she walked back from the toilet and up towards Ray.

"What's going on here then?" Chris said, looking at the tall woman towering over her.

"She is just leaving, I think," Ray said, turning his back and signalling Bodie to carry on with his stretch and exercise. He had no more interest in the woman and just left it to Chris to sort out.

Chris was standing in front of her target, but only came to just above her breasts, the woman had to look down at her.

"Get out of my way," she said, with a disgusted tone in her voice and a look to match.

"You are in my way, bitch, so you get out of the fucking way," Chris told her, looking her straight in the eye and making the woman nervous and annoyed at the same time.

"You little people are disgusting. I have wiped better off my shoe than both of you stupid creatures." Her lip curled as she gave Chris a look up and down.

"Do you realise how fucking false and stupid you look? False tits, false teeth, false hair, makeup to the fucking eyeballs; if we take it all away, what is left? Oh yes, a lump of useless shit." Chris glared at this woman, hating her more and more as the moments passed.

The standoff was broken when Ray walked past and smiled at the tall, attractive woman, but said to Chris, "When your ready, babe, we have work to do."

He went to the car and let Bodie in, then he walked around and got in himself. He looked over and saw Chris saying something to the woman. He could not hear what she was saying, but the worried look on the face of her victim said it all. She was left standing there as Chris cockily walked back to the car. She got in and didn't look back as they drove away.

"Friend of yours, was she?" Chris asked, settling back in her seat. She felt better now that she had stretched and let off a little steam.

"She wanted to be, but what the hell, she is a woman."

"Was she? That much fucking surgery going on there, love, it wouldn't surprise me if it wasn't a man once."

"What did you say to her?" Ray asked, looking over with a little smile at his small but powerful lady.

"Just said if she didn't want to see the inside of her own fucking arsehole to fuck off."

"Oh, you are so polite sometimes."

"I know, I get it from you." She glanced at him with a smile and they both had a nice quiet thought to themselves as they drove on down the road and into the morning light breaking down the darkness of the night.

"I don't like the way this has gone or, in fact, is going, Chris. Something is very wrong," Ray finally said, breaking the companionable silence.

"I was just thinking the same. It has been a mess from start to finish. And I still don't understand what Xander wants with the shifter," Chris wondered, glancing over at Ray.

"Or is it the shifter who wants Xander? Who the hell is controlling who there? Xander has the power to crush us whenever he wants and this shifter can summon up an army of the dead. So why the hell have they not done it?"

"What are they waiting for?" Chris frowned as she thought about it for a moment.

"You're good on dates and the such, is there a special time coming up, some ritual or something?" Ray was grasping at straws and knew it.

Chris shook her head. She was thinking herself, but could not come up with anything.

"Our child?" she asked painfully after a few moments.

"I don't understand." Ray shook his head in confusion.

"Why did they take our child? What reason would they have to do that, or was it just because they could?"

"I don't know? How could they use that against us?"

"We have been over this. I don't know." She shook her head and wished she had not brought it up. It was still too painful for her to take at the moment.

The day was rising and the air was very fresh and clean. There were still not many cars or people about, but that would soon change. For now they enjoyed the relatively calm roads and quiet morning drive.

Ray was not sure what he would do when he got to where he was heading, but at this point it was the only thing he could think of. He was out of practice and had slowed down these past few years that he had been away from the fight. He wanted all the advantages he could get. He knew he would not be bothered at the farmhouse and would have a clear battleground if he needed it.

What would come for him, he was not sure, but he had the sword and this made him feel much more powerful. He also had his trusted best friend Bodie and he had the woman who he loved next to him. It made a formidable force, he thought, and it made him feel a little more secure and little more confident about the situation he was going into and what he would have to do to come out the other end of it.

CHAPTER 17

The two litre engine hummed, easing the car around the corner to head up the hill to the farmhouse. Ray looked forward and stayed focused ready at all times.

Chris sat up in her seat, ready. She looked around, familiarising herself with the surroundings once again, as they pulled into the deserted area through the two pillars where the gates had hung.

Ray drove the car over the uneven ground slowly up to the old barn area. He stopped and looked over at Chris who was staring back at him.

"Into battle," he said. Getting out of the car he stretched and lifted his arms above his head, smelling the fresh midmorning air.

Walking round to the back of the car, Ray opened the hatchback and lifted the tent from its screwed-up position. He noticed the sword sitting under it. He stopped for a moment, then took the heavy weapon from the back. He lifted it and watched it gleam and shimmer in the sunlight; a truly magnificent weapon, he thought admiringly.

Chris got out and let Bodie out of the back door. They both stretched also and took deep breaths of air. Chris watched Ray behind the car with the sword. The length of the blade was just right for Ray's size. It could have been made for him and, in a way, she supposed it was.

Bodie wondered off and was marking out the area, so Chris took this moment to look around the deserted place. It still felt cold even thought it was a bright, sunny day. It was a dead place and she hated it, even more than she'd hated it before.

She noticed Bodie sniffing the dead body of the giant that she and Ray had killed days before. She didn't want to go up to it and turned away, staring out across the way to the hole where the shifter originally came from. She walked past Ray and towards the rockery of stone around the hole and stood, looking at it.

She peered into the darkness and was instantly shocked at what she saw. The face of Xander looking back up at her. Before she could scream or even move, he was up and out of the hole. He grabbed her around the neck with one large, powerful hand and silently lifted her up in the air, grinning at her with hate in his eyes as he did.

She was unable to make a noise; he was squeezing the very life out of her. Levitating above the ground, he looked over at Ray, who had just noticed what was happening. He had shouted for Bodie and was running towards them, the sword held ready in his right hand.

Xander lifted his other hand and signalled Ray to stop, but he kept coming. Xander took his hand and placed it on Chris's head, threatening to snap her neck.

Ray reluctantly stopped dead in his tracks with Bodie by his side, growling at him.

Laughing in the voice of the shifter, Xander's eyes rolled back and he lifted Chris higher, about to rip her head from her shoulders.

Ray shouted, but saw in that split second Chris's eyes flicker open. She jabbed with all her might into Xander's eyes and kicked out with the little strength she had.

It was just enough to distract him and make him lose his sight of Ray and loosen his grip on Chris. Which was just enough time for Ray to cover the few yards to them and plunge the sword into Xander's stomach.

The blade cut deeply, penetrating the flesh and guts savagely. Chris was awkwardly dropped to the ground and managed to roll off to one side, gasping for the much needed air and clutching her throat, which felt as though it was on fire.

Bodie had pounced and was ripping into Xander's neck, causing him to stagger back. Ray pushed the blade further in and twisted it with all the strength he could muster. Bodie was knocked away and went flying through the air, landing on his feet and running back within seconds.

Ray threw a jab at Xander's throat, knocking his head back and giving him his target area. He pulled the sword and swung it high. However, as soon as the sword was out of Xander's throat, his expression changed and he flew backwards and up out of reach.

The sword shook violently in Ray's hand. It was was uncontrollable and aggressive and he was unable to stop it. Confused, he looked up at Xander, who was smiling down at him, and then looked at Chris, who was on her knees, coughing and trying to swallow and get her windpipe working again.

Bodie growled and barked at Xander, who was out of his reach.

Ray had no idea what was happening. The sword continued to shake and he had to hold it with both hands so not to drop it. He looked at the blade and saw the shiny metal had a flaw in it; a darkness moving the length of the blade, like a shadow moving up and down. A darkness trying to escape from the sword it was trapped in.

The shifter was trapped, Ray had caught and entombed it in the sword. He looked at Xander and could see this is was what had happened Xander was now free of the shifter and Ray had it in the sword.

He looked at the hole and threw the blade down it. A scream of anguish and pain rung out as he did; the whole earth shook as the sword hit the bottom of the dark hole.

He then dashed to Chris's side, trying to help her. She had colour back in her cheeks, but was still struggling to breath.

The hole was collapsing in on itself, sealing back up and encasing the sword and what it had captured back down into the depths of the earth.

Xander let out a cry of joy and a laugh of menace. He stared down at Chris and opened his mouth at her. Ray looked around to see how far he was away from the car and his weaponry.

Chris stood up on her own two feet and pushed Ray away from her, not in a nasty way, but in a way to tell him to leave her and get on with what he had to do. She was breathing heavily and gasping a bit. She was recovering quickly; she knew she had to.

Ray turned and faced Xander just as the ground stopped shaking and the hole was again filled and sealed.

Bodie spun on the spot and looked at the car. He noticed the ground move, the car shake and the four fighting men with long poles appear from the ground. All were dressed in black and all had fighting physiques. And they were all staring at Ray.

By now, the shaking had subsided and the car had dropped in the ditch that had appeared around the four men.

They stood strong and looked at Ray, each with a large wooden pole in their hands. Each pole was about six feet long and each man knew how to use the Bo staffs to great effectiveness.

They all swung the poles around and rested them under their arm with the ends pointing out, ending in a cry that would curdle the blood of any mortal man. The dirt dropped from their bodies and they shook it off.

Ray spun and saw his enemies as they stood, four abreast, looking at him.

He saw he had no chance of getting to the car, nowhere to run. He had nothing to fight with, Chris was injured and Xander was behind him. All in all, he was not in a good position. Bodie, as ever, was by his side, staring at the four men who were slowly walking towards them.

They began to split and form a semi-circle. Ray knew what they were doing and had no choice but to let them do it. They soon were circling Bodie and Ray one at each side and one behind and one directly in front. They held their poles out and stared with black, evil eyes at Ray.

Xander had lowered down and grabbed Chris by the back of her neck, lifting her again like a rag doll into the air. She had no strength to fight him off and had to just hang there painfully, watching helplessly as Ray was surrounded.

The standoff was silent and Ray was trying to eye the weakest link, any chance he could find. However they all looked very skillful and were not going to be beaten easily, if at all.

Ray took a deep breath and slowly looked behind him at the pole fighter standing there. They all seemed to be exactly the same distance from him, so none would be the first in line for his attack.

They all suddenly moved and shifted into a fighting stance, holding their wooden poles in both hands. Their faces changed from a blankness to a look of sheer hate.

Bodie growled and just looked at the one in front of him. Ray instinctively knew Bodie would go for that one, so concentrated on the other three. He could see they were going to fight as a unit and not as individuals. This made it all the more difficult to control. He slowly put his hand in his side jacket pocket and slipped the knuckle duster over his right fingers and gripped it in his fist.

He pulled his hand out quickly as the four men moved towards him as one. Bodie pounced for his target. Ray dropped to one knee and, faster than he ever had before, pulled his knife from his boot and threw it at the man in front of him, hitting him directly in the throat. The blade dug in deep and severed the windpipe. Blood instantly gushed from the artery the knife had severed and the pole fighter was down.

Bodie was not as lucky and was hit violently with the pole across the head, reeling him off to the side with a yelp.

Chris watched with dread in her eyes; she could see the odds were stacked up against Ray and she can do nothing to help him. Xander's grip tightened and she almost passed out with the pain he was inflicting.

The pain of the pole swiping and hitting him was shocking; it made his head rock back and the pain belted through him like a bolt of lightening. The first one was bad but the second one caught him on the other side of the head and he went, stunned, off to the side.

He had to keep moving, he knew that, but his strength and consciousness was diminishing rapidly. The poles came down again and he was hit across the back. Rolling into the fighter, he tried to knock him off his balance but the pole fighter was too experienced, jumping and over Ray. He jabbed his pole down end first into Ray's side, making him scream out in agony.

Bodie was up and shook himself off. He was more cautious this time and barked and growled at the pole fighter in front of him, who turned calmly and held his pole out to face Bodie.

The other two brought their poles up again and brought them down with a sickening thud across Ray's back. He slumped down on the floor in pain.

Bodie snapped at the wooden pole being jabbed at him. He spun around and pounced again, but not at the man in front of him, this time he went for one at his side, who was lifting his pole to bring it down on Ray's head.

The weight of the dog brought the man down and saved Ray a savage and more than likely fatal blow to his temple. Ripping as fast and as savagely as he could, Bodie tore at the man's throat, pulling the windpipe out. He paid for his bravery when the other two brought the weight of their poles down on the dog's back and head.

Ray had just enough time to roll away and grab a much needed breath in an attempt to stop his head from spinning.

Chris tried to scream. The pain she was feeling at seeing both Bodie and Ray taking a beating they could not survive was unbearable. Although it was a horrible sight for her, she found that she couldn't pull her eyes away.

Bodie was badly hurt and tried to run away, but the pole crashed down onto his back and dropped him painfully to the ground. Another pole jabbed violently into his side, making him yelp out in excruciating pain.

Ray screamed as he saw what had happened. He staggered to his feet and dropped again. He was dazed and in trouble, but the sight of the beating Bodie was taking forced him to his feet.

He rolled over to the first pole fighter that he killed with the knife. He took his knife from his throat and ran with the little strength he had straight at the pole fighter nearest to him. He rammed with all his weight into him and, although he got hit again with the pole, he managed to run through it and stab the man hard in the chest with his knife.

As he dropped, Ray fell on top of him, still hold of the knife in his hand as the man squirmed and fought from under him. Crying out, Ray twisted the knife and pushed it deeper into the wound. He looked over at the lifeless beaten body of his dog and pushed the knife harder. Blood splattered his face as he grunted out the last bit of energy he had.

The pain he felt this time dazed him. The pole caught him full in the face and reeled him back flat onto his back. The last pole fighter was there, standing above him. Ray was helpless; he had no more power to stand, to fight, or to move. He rasped as he breathed deeply and awkwardly. The pole fighter raised the pole like an axe and held it poised above him, smiling.

Chris tried again to cry out but nothing happened, her throat had given up on her. She saw Bodie battered and still. Ray was down and the pole fighter was about to deliver the final fatal blow.

Xander laughed and pulled her away, turning her to face him. He grinned with the devil in his deep black eyes as he moved away from the scene that had unfolded in front of them. All she could see was his eyes as they some how drifted back and away.

She heard the pole crash down and a deep thud as it hit. She closed her eyes and, at that moment, her heart died. Ray was dead. The man she had planned to spend the rest of her life with had been beaten to death with a wooden pole and she had no chance of helping him or ever seeing him again. She began to lose consciousness and the cold and the darkness followed. She was out cold and at the mercy of Xander.

CHAPTER 18

Ray, however, had one more trick up his sleeve. He had lifted his right fist up just as the pole came crashing down, reinforced this with his left hand around his right wrist. The knuckle duster took the full brunt of the pole and stopped it inches from his head.

He kicked out at the man's groin and caught him square in the testicles, making him freeze for a second in absolute shock. He dropped his pole and Ray reached over and took it. Using his last bit of strength, he swung it hard at the man's head, hitting him and sending him off to the side.

He dropped the pole. He felt sick and dizzy. He looked over at Bodie's lifeless body and dropped his head. He passed out face down in the dirt, blood weeping from the gaping gash in his skull.

The scene was violent and bloody, bodies laid out in the dirt. No one moved and even the air was still. It was as if time warped and this was suddenly another place and another time. The battle did not belong in this century, did not belong in this world.

***

Chris did not know how long she had been unconscious. She slowly opened her eyes and winced at the pain in her throat. She could not swallow or move her neck, it was too stiff. She had to hunch and hold it still while moving her whole upper body around to see where she was.

The room was cold and had a damp stone floor with bare stone walls. The only light she could see was coming from under the thick wooden door that was firmly shut at one end of the small cellar-like room.

She shivered in the cold and took a breath of air which was damp and smelled putrid. In the dark and cold and in pain, she lowered her body back down and laid still. She could not sit or take the weight of her head on her neck, it was too painful. She tried to conserve her energy and rest as best she could.

She closed her eyes, but they sprang open again as she remembered the sight of Ray and Bodie laying dead in the dirt. Her heart contracted with pain and sorrow. She fought back the tears and hurt, trying unsuccessfully to stay focused.

This was the end. She had no strength to fight her way out and no will to go on now that she had no one to go on with. The time she had spent with Ray was the best she had ever had and now it was gone. Ended violently.

The thoughts sickened her and the sorrow was too much to bear. She sobbed silently in the damp, cold place she found herself in. She had no idea what her fate would be and, right now, she didn't care.

***

The faint noise of voices stirred in Ray's head.

"Is he dead?"

"What has happened?"

He could not make out who it was; he wasn't even sure if they were really there or just in his mind.

"What about the dog?"

"We need a stretcher."

He heard the voices but could not move. He couldn't see or feel anything, he wasn't even sure where he was.

"We will have to pull the car out of the ditch."

"Let's get out of here, I don't like it."

"Where's Chris?"

Ray tried to raise himself up, but nothing happened. It was dark and he could just hear the faint voices in the distance.

"I will tow the car out and you drive it."

"He is in a bad way. Is the dog dead?"

Ray felt completely helpless; unable to move or even make a sound, although he tried with all his might. He listened carefully but the voices seemed to have gone and it was silent now.

He could feel the creeping anxiety. He heard them mention her and he realized that he couldn't feel her. As in tune as they were, he had become accustomed to always feeling her inside himself. So much that he even knew her mood, without her having to say a word.

And now the feeling was gone. Chris was gone.

Frustrated and frightened, he shouted for her, though no sound came from his lips.

***

The door swung open violently, hitting the wall with a thud that startled Chris, and she felt a jolt of pain rip though her neck as she jumped at the noise. Looking over to the door and trying to accustom her eyes to the light now streaming in, she blinked several times and narrowed her eyes to try and make out who was there.

Tall and looking as attractive as ever was the woman from the service station that had talked to Ray and who Chris had savaged with her tongue.

She looked down and smirked at her then, taking one step in, she lifted her foot and kicked Chris hard in the shoulder with her high heel digging in to her flesh. She laughed as Chris rolled off in tremendous pain, coming to rest curled up and looking pitifully up at this woman towering above her.

"Not so tough now, are we? You are so stupid. We have been following you ever since you started and we have been using you all the time to get what we needed. You and that thick bastard gave us exactly what we wanted. And now you are going to serve my master in any way that he desires, you fucking wench. Not so cocky now, are we bitch? You are going to serve the master and I am going to make sure you do and enjoy the vile things he wants to do to you."

She cocked her head back and laughed a laugh that Chris instantly hated. It was a 'get on your nerves' laugh and one she wanted to shut up. She made a mental note that she would one day.

The light was blocked out once again as a large figure appeared in the doorway.

"Leave!" Xander's voice boomed in the small confined space and bounced off the stone walls.

The woman bowed her head instantly and shuffled out of the room past him and away. Chris looked up at him bearing down on her.

"You have nothing, no one. All you have now is me, and you will serve me and do as I command."

He moved slowly into the room and looked down at her intensely, with eyes that turned black as she looked at them. She was helpless to do anything and she knew it. Her power was sapped and her position was not good, to say the least.

Xander looked down and then lifted his head and smiled at her, before saying in the same powerful voice, "You did exactly what I wanted. So predictable, so stupid and so blind. Did you really think you would have a chance against me?"

He stopped smiling and his face twisted in disgust as he turned and left the room, slamming the door shut as he did. She heard the bolt lock and secure the wooden door from outside and she was alone again.

She shivered at the damp coldness of the floor. Painfully, she got to her hands and knees. However, her neck was so sore and weak that it caused her agony and she had to rest it again on her hands as she laid back down on the stone floor. She was trapped and was left to await her fate.

***

"Ray can you hear me Ray?"

The voice was distant but becoming louder. He tried to open his eyes but one refused to move and the other just opened a little. He saw through the half-open eye the face of Jan looking worriedly at him as she leaned over him in her white coat.

He opened his mouth to speak but nothing came out except a dry gurgle and a slight cough.

"Don't try to speak, just nod your head if you can hear me."

He nodded slightly while looking at her, his eye focusing a little better now.

"Okay, just listen. You are in a bad way and I have done what I can. You are in my clinic at the moment, but we are moving you to Darius' tonight. I am going to sedate you for the journey, so you won't know anything about it until you wake again .

Seeing his questioning look, she continued, "You are badly beaten and have a concussion. How the hell you don't have any broken bones I don't know, but you are going to be sore for a while.

She saw his eyes narrow at her suspiciously and knew what he was thinking, answering his implied question. "Darius and I followed you and managed to save you, but only just, I must say."

Ray tried to move and speak. His body shook with pain as he moved just a few inches. He tried to speak, but Jan stopped him, touching him gently on the shoulder.

"Chris?" he managed to spit out before sighing and moaning out the agony he was in.

"You have to rest, Ray. You cannot move and should not do so for some time. Bodie is at the vet's and in a similar state as you, but he is alive." She smiled at him and hoped it would comfort him for the time being.

He again tried to speak, but this time he just grunted in pain and didn't form a word.

Jan smiled at him and walked from the room. He watched as she went, then slowly he turned his head. He could see he was in a small room; very basic, but clean, warm and tidy. He had been made comfortable, but wanted to get up and he tried, realising that it was useless.

His battered body refused to comply with his request so he stayed still and the ache, the pain began to make itself known. His whole body was screaming at him, though the pain in his head was worse, like the most severe headache he had ever had, multiplied a hundred times. He closed his good eye and quietly suffered.

The only thing that made him feel any better was knowing that Bodie was alive.

But this was overshadowed by not knowing about Chris. He winced at the pain as he moved his head a little too much to the side to look at the door where Jan had gone. He wanted to get up, wanted to make her tell him where Chris was, but he knew he was in no shape to do anything, so he conceded and stayed still, allowing his body to heal. It was all he could do.

***

Darius looked up at Jan as she came back into her office and sat at her well-kept and tidy desk. She leaned back in her black leather chair and looked at Darius looking at her as he put his cup of coffee down on a coaster on her desk.

"He is awake, but very weak," she said.

"What did you say to him?"

"I told him we are moving him to your place tonight. I also told him not to worry and to get some rest," she replied, shrugging her shoulders.

"Did you tell him about Chris?"

"No. I didn't say anything about her at all. He asked though," she said sadly.

"It's just terrible. I don't know what to do, Jan."

"We need to see if we can find her. He won't be still for long and when he gets going are we going to be able to stop him? We both know he's in no fit state, but what can we do?"

"Wonder what happened out there. If we could of only got there sooner." Darius shook his head and sighed.

"Doesn't anyone know anything?"

"It's all quiet and, to be honest, what can we do against Xander? The only man who had a chance is in the next room battered to a pulp."

"He will recover, he is strong."

"It's not him I am worried about." A sadness came across Darius' face and he bowed his head slightly as he thought about where Chris could be. He wondered if she was laying somewhere in pain or if she was even alive.

"Come, Darius, this is not like you. We have to stay strong, if not for us, for him in there. He is the only chance we have. He is the only chance Chris has."

"Yes, I know you're right, I'm sorry. We might know more when we can talk to him and find out what happened. How long do you think it will be before he can tell us anything?"

"Well, it has been two days and I still have him sedated somewhat; no doubt the pain is still crushing. We will see what he is like tomorrow when he wakes at your place. I think he will be up and about soon, his spirit is too strong to keep him down too long, and we do need to get him moving."

"I have to go and see about his dog. They are having trouble with him, they cannot control him. I think he needs to see his master to calm down. Right now they are knocking him out with sedatives to keep him quiet."

"tell them to bring him to your place sedated and, when he wakes, Ray will be with him. He is just mending like his master. Cracked ribs and bad bruising they said, didn't they?"

"Good job they are both as hard as nails."

"It is a very good job they are so strong and hard, yes. Any other man would have been dead by now. I just hope Chris is all right. I am sure we will find her."

"Yes she is strong and can take care of herself. If there is a way to survive she will find it."

***

Bodie slowly opened his eyes. He was laying on a carpet in a warm room, different from the vet's kennel he had been in. He recognised the smells and looked around the place through his sleepy eyes.

He looked up at the bed and saw Ray laying there, sniffing his familiar scent. It lifted him immensely and he tried to stand, but the sedative and the stiffness of his beaten body made it slow and painful. He still got to his feet and, although he was unsteady, he walked to the bed and, with his tail was wagging, his ears back and his eyes full of love and relief, he nosed Ray's hand then licked it.

Ray turned his head and a smile broke across his swollen face. He lifted his hand and stroked his trusted dog. They were both glad to be reunited. Bodie tried to get closer and yelped with the pain but jumped up and landed paws first on top of Ray, making him squirm in agony. He didn't mind, though, it was Bodie and he could do anything he wanted.

Bodie licked Ray's face and Ray put both arms around his big dog, hugging and kissing him back. This was a special moment and it was just the medicine that they both needed.

They were both in pain from the reunion, but it was overridden by their happiness and the love they had for each other. They lay side by side, enjoying the warmth.

Now he just had to get up and moving so that he could go and find the other love of his life and get her safe.

CHAPTER 19

Chris was shivering from the cold. The pain in her throat and neck had eased slightly, but she was weak from lack of food. The only water they had given her for two days was a small cup, half-filled. The rumbling in her stomach was constant and she struggled to keep warm. The dampness had seeped into her clothes.

At least she could sit up now and did not have to lay all the time. She stood and rotated her neck around slowly, trying to get it moving again, and exercised. Walking to the door, she put her ear to the wood and listened, hearing nothing.

Although her eyes had grown accustomed to the darkness she still could see very little, but she took great notice every time the door was opened to look around the room and as much of the outside as she could.

The hall directly outside of the door was warm looking and had painted walls. She could also smell the scent of burning essence, though she couldn't put her finger on what the scent was.

She froze as the noise of footsteps came closer and she backed off from the door. Ray had always told her not to let the enemy know what state you are in if you are captured, do not let them know how good or bad you are, just stay neutral and ordinary. Conserve your strength and take any opportunity you can. Her neck was getting better but she still pretended it was bad and remained silent.

The door was kicked open with a thud and the light hurt her eyes, causing her to lift her hand to shield them from it.

"Come with me, whore. We have to get you cleaned up, you stink of piss and you're smelling the place out," the woman from the service station said to her. She was the one who had been bringing Chris the half cup of water and she nicknamed her Skank.

Chris slowly walked past her. She was prodded from behind by Skank and pushed out of the room. Chris took in as much information as she could, a stair landing of sorts. She was faced with some steps leading up and it was the only way to go, so she started to walk up them.

The air became damp and when she pushed open the wooden door at the top, it opened out into a large kitchen that was outdated and unused. She looked to the left and saw her first daylight through the small windows.

"That way, you little whore," Skank said and pushed her violently towards another door at the other side of the kitchen.

Chris stayed calm and said nothing; this was not the time to argue. She had to get her bearings and see if there was an exit for escape.

The door opened before Chris got to it and another tall, attractive woman, much the same as Skank, stood there looking at Chris disgustedly. She pointed to a small shower room to the side of the main hall she was now in, which was grand and expensive-looking, much nicer than the kitchen.

The front door was about five yards away. She thought about dashing for it but decided against it and instead went into the small shower room, hearing the door close behind her.

She was happy for the chance to shower and go to the toilet. There were clothes also that were about her size and she picked them up and looked at them. Jeans and a small top with a jumper; not what she would have chosen, but they were dry and clean so she didn't grumble.

She relished the feeling of the hot water cascading down her body, washing the dirt, the damp and the ache from her. She washed well and cleaned her hair only with a bar of soap but it was better than nothing.

She came out and used one of the two towels to dry herself. Feeling much better after the shower, she got dressed quickly. She went to the sink and turned on the tap. She took a long drink of water and then did the same again, swallowing it deep, then went back down for a third time.

She stretched and rubbed her neck, taking this bit of time to move and get her joints working again. She felt much more invigorated now that she was clean and fresh again.

The door was pushed open and Skank came in. She grabbed her by the shoulder and roughly dragged her from the room and pushed her towards the stairs leading up to the second floor. Chris again said nothing and tilted her head, pretending her neck was still hurting more that is was.

She was led into a bedroom and pushed towards the double bed situated in the middle of the large room. It was very basic but much more comfortable then the cellar she had been.

"The master and friends are having you for fun soon, so they want you ready," she said, smiling a bitchy smile.

Chris did not let that faze her at all, she was just glad to be out of the cellar. She turned and walked to the bed and sat down, saying nothing.

Skank left and locked the door behind her. Chris stood and went to the door, listening intently. She could her the footsteps going away into the distance. She moved quickly and peered out of the window.

The wooden frames were securely locked, not that she had a chance of escape anyway; it was sheer drop down and she would never make it from this height. All she could see were fields and more fields out into the distance.

Turning back, she looked into the wardrobe in the corner, finding it was empty. She did the same with the drawers at the side of the bed, finding them empty as well. She found nothing under the bed either. She knew they would not put her somewhere where she could find something to fight or escape with.

Looking around once more, she went to the bed and laid down. Her body felt better and her neck was improving.

She closed her eyes and thought of Ray, which made her heart sink. She opened her eyes again, took a deep breath and sighed and just lay there, alone with her own thoughts.

***

When Darius came into Ray's room, he was surprised to see him sitting on the edge of the bed. He looked up and stared at Darius blankly.

"Ray, you should be resting," Darius said as he came in with a bowl of soup and two rolls of bread.

"Where is Chris? Why are you not telling me? Is she hurt?" He winced slightly, he was still not able to move his bottom jaw fully yet.

"Eat this and get your strength back, then we can discuss other things." Darius smiled but stopped when he saw the look Ray was giving him.

He put the soup bowl and bread down. Ray reached out and grabbed hold of him, pulling him towards him, close to his face.

"I will not ask you again."

"We don't know. We searched everywhere but could not find her. We have no idea where she is," Darius said, standing back upright as Ray let him go.

Ray's face saddened. He looked down at Bodie then back at Darius saying, "Xander took her. He had hold of her, he must have taken her."

"Xander was there? Is he the one who you fought with? There were four men around you and a giant of man too, but he looked like he had been there longer."

"He had yes. The four were summoned by Xander and he took Chris away from me. I am going to get her back."

He slid off the bed and stood up. He steadied himself and Darius could see he was in discomfort but gave him a little space by backing off.

"You are still weak, Ray, you need to get your strength back. You cannot go anywhere yet, you're not ready."

"Xander has Chris and I am not fucking waiting around!"

"You will play right into his hands. You can not fight anyone in the state you're in at the moment. And how will that help Chris?"

Ray conceded, knowing that Darius was right. He looked at the soup and up at Darius again.

"Well, get me some better food than that. I want some meat and proper food to get me going again."

He walked out of the room and went to the bathroom. Bodie watched him from the floor and picked his ears up, listening to every sound that Ray made. The toilet flushed and he came back in, arching his back and stretching it as much as he dare. It was very sore and he was still stiff, but he was determined to get up and going as soon as possible.

"I will make you some dinner then," Darius said as he left the room.

Ray sat on the bed and looked at the soup, lifting the spoon to taste it. Unimpressed, he broke the two bread rolls up into pieces and put them in the soup, then put the bowl on the floor. Bodie slowly stood and came over. He smelt it then ate it, lapping up the whole lot.

Ray stood and walked to the window. He peered out and saw his car parked up below him. The roof had a gaping hole in it, the duck tape was gone.

"How are you feeling, Ray, are you still dizzy?" a woman's voice asked him from the doorway.

He turned and saw it was Jan, looking at him with concern. She came in and smiled down at Bodie as she walked past him. She looked at the gash on Ray's head, inspecting the stitches that she had put in there days before.

She then looked into his eyes, asking, "Can you see all right? Are you still getting headaches?"

"I will live. Thank you for what you have done."

"My pleasure. You were lucky we came along. If we had not got to you when we did, you would be dead now, both of you," she nodded down towards Bodie.

"Why did you come along? Why the hell were you following us anyway?" Ray asked, pulling his head away from her hands.

"Darius and I were very concerned and thought you needed help. We *were* following you and I am glad we did."

"Well, yeah, I suppose." He looked back out of the window at his car again.

"Darius has a friend who owns a garage and he is going to fix your car. You are getting a sunroof put in. You have a hole now, you will have sunroof by tomorrow." She smiled at him.

"I used to have a sunroof in it. I filled it in and welded a plate across it," Ray said, remembering

"You filled a sunroof in? I have never heard of that before, I didn't think you could do that."

"You can do anything if you really put your mind to it."

"I will not argue there. It is good to have a positive attitude and keep forging ahead."

"I'm going to get Chris. Will you help me?" Ray turned and looked at her, she had a serious look on her face.

"Yes, any way I can, but you are badly beaten and you need to heal and get your strength back."

"So everyone keeps telling me. How the hell do we know what he is doing to her and what he wants her for, if she is even still alive." He clenched his fists and ground his teeth at the thought of what he had just said.

"If he wanted to kill her, he would have done it there and then, surely. Why take her away just to kill her? He must want her for a reason, I think."

"What is that, what reason would he want her for?"

"Well she is quite a catch in the dark circles and I would think he has plans for her." She regretted what she had said as soon as she said it and bit her lip involuntary.

"What plans? What do you mean, the dark circles?" Ray asked intensely through gritted teeth.

"Xander is all powerful and he likes to show off. Chris will be like a trophy to him, something to exhibit and to parade in front of his kind."

"How do we find him? How do I get to Xander? Your lot must know where he is or can find out where he is, surely."

"I think you have the power to find him yourself, Ray."

"I have tried with my board many times, but I have never been able to get to him." Ray shook his head and walked up to Jan. He stood in front of her and she looked up at him.

"You're a good woman, Jan, and I thank you for all your help. I won't forget it and if there is anything I can ever do for you, don't hesitate to ask."

She smiled a little schoolgirl smile and put her hand to her mouth, blinking her eyes a little slower than normal.

"You should not say things like that to a girl, Ray. If you do want to do something for me, listen to my advice and let me get you back fighting fit and then go and kill the fucker." She smiled and looked at him, waiting for his answer.

"Deal. And I will bring you his head on a plate."

"Just your word you have done it will do."

"What do you want me to do? How can I get back in to shape and moving again?" He stretched and arched his back, sighing out at the ache he experienced.

"I will get you right. We will stretch you and get you working again, but it will take a little time. You are the only one who can do it. You're strong and determined so let's stop pissing about and get working, shall we?"

Ray smiled at her, although it was a crooked one. He liked Jan and was going to do as she asked.

***

Skank came into the room with a tray and dropped it down next to the bed on the small table. It had an apple and some sandwiches on it with half a cup of water. She looked at Chris, who sat up and wanted to dive for the food she was so hungry, but controlled herself and just looked at the woman she hated in front of her.

"You not saying much bitch. You were all mouth before, what's wrong? You scared?" She smiled and put her face closer to Chris's. "You should be because you are going to be the entertainment for the master and his friends when they arrive. You will be ripped apart and I will be there watching and loving every minute of it. What was it you said to me, if I don't want to see the inside of my arse I had better shut up and fuck off? Well, we will be seeing much more of you than that when they have finished with you."

Chris said nothing, just wanting the food, so she pointed to her throat and opened her mouth, signalling she could not say anything, though she knew she could if she wanted to.

"What, can't speak? Fucking good job or I might have had to teach you a lesson in manners, bitch." Skank walked back out of the room and locked the door.

Chris sat up on the edge of the bed and devoured the food within minutes. She was so hungry that it went straight down. She barely tasted it and didn't really care, so long as it filled her stomach or at least some of it. She ate the apple, core and all, and drank the water.

Wiping her mouth with the back of her hand, she stood up and went to the window, looking out across the fields and wondering where she was.

She closed her eyes and saw Ray's face, smiling at her. She remembered his piercing blue eyes and blunt attitude, his strong features and striking good looks, his no-messing-about way of doing things and his old fashioned values.

She smiled as she remembered the times they had spent together and the happiness they had shared. She frowned at the battles they had fought and the terrifying ordeals they had been through. She remembered the first time she saw him, she remembered the first time he kissed her and took her in his strong arms. Opening her eyes again she sighed and sniffled, tears welling in her eyes.

She turned back into the room. Standing there, she looked around, rotating her neck and rubbing it with her hands. It was loosening more and felt a lot better than it had done days before. She stretched out and went back and laid on the bed.

***

Bodie sniffed the tree in the park while Ray stood nearby watching him. The night had begun to close in and the park was deserted, just the way he wanted and liked it. He had took Bodie out for a walk to get moving again. He was painful and stiff and everything ached but he and Bodie were fighting to at least get onto the road to recovery.

Moving his head from side to side, he stretched his muscles and rotated his head and then his shoulders. Feeling was returning, but slowly. He breathed in and it didn't hurt as much as it had done before. The headache was still there, but the extra strong painkillers Jan had given him took a lot of it away.

Bodie was not too bad. He had been given something by the vet and it seemed to make him into a new dog. Ray wondered ruefully if they could give him the same stuff.

He walked past Bodie and up the small hill, breathing deeply as he watched Bodie come up the hill to join him. They slowly strolled back to the house and his thoughts wandered to Chris. How much of an effect she had on him, the way she always stuck by him and the way she always fought by his side. He could trust her like no other woman on earth and he was going to do everything he could to get her back.

He kept the thought that she was alive in his head just so he could think straight and work out how to get to her. If he didn't he knew he would be no good to her or himself.

CHAPTER 20

The next day was drizzly and damp, dull and depressing, but it did not match Ray's mood at all. He was doing press-ups and gritting his teeth through the pain, but he wanted to get moving, wanted to get strong and wanted to find Chris.

The pain killers Jan had given him were doing wonders. He was not sure what they were, but they did the trick. He moved much better and was much more flexible than he had been since the fight.

He came down the stairs and ate the breakfast Darius gladly made for him. He sat across from him and sipped his coffee as Ray finished the mound of food on his plate.

He took a deep swig of his tea and looked at Darius saying, "Any biscuits in the house?"

"No, you have eaten them all. I will get some more when I go shopping," Darius told him, smiling.

"I need to find out where he is keeping her. How do I do that, do you think?" Ray asked, leaning back in his chair.

"If you can not detect him, then maybe you can detect those around him or those serving him?"

"I don't know who they are, do I?" Ray said, picking a piece of food from the gap in his mouth where a tooth had been knocked out years before.

"If Jan and I are right, he will want to show her off and, when he does, he will want his people around him; the high priestess, the black wizard and the evil horde he commands."

"But where, where is the fucker? That is what I need to know."

"Ray, sometimes I wonder how the hell you got so far. No disrespect, but you have the power to detect these things, you always have. Kaden helps you though your Ouija. If there is that much evil accumulated in one spot, don't you think your board, Kaden and you will be able to pinpoint it? I am sure you can." Darius had a serious tone because he knew Ray would do just that and be gone. He also knew Ray was not fighting fit yet but it would not stop him.

Looking at Darius for several moments, Ray said nothing, then just nodded his head with a satisfied look on his face. He took another drink of his tea and set the cup down.

"You said you could track her by her mobile phone, why can't you do that now?"

"The phone has to be switched on. I don't think she would be allowed her phone, do you?"

"Just a thought. Is my car ready today? I will pay you for your trouble, I owe you much but I will pay you for what I can and thank you again for what you have done."

"You owe me nothing, it is we who owe you, Ray. The whole world owes you, they just don't know it."

"Well, it's better than me owing the whole world, isn't it? I don't understand this world and the people who live in it; the arrogance, the greed, the selfishness, the disrespect, the lack of honour and courage and..." He stopped and shook his head with disgusted look on his face.

"It is the way of the world, Ray, and you won't change it. The place is a time bomb and sooner or later it will explode."

"Yeah, you're probably right. When is he bringing my car back?"

"Just after dinner, he said."

"I will find them tonight and go and get her back," he said in a matter-of-fact way.

Darius didn't understand but had learned not to question. He nodded a yes before saying, "We want to help and want you to let us help. Don't say you don't need it, because you do."

"Yes, I do, and I would appreciate all the help I can get, Darius, but it will be too dangerous for you to come with me."

"You need more time. Do you think you are fit enough?" he asked doubtfully.

"I don't have any more time, I have left it too long already. The drugs Jan is giving me are working and I feel okay again, well, almost okay again." He shrugged his shoulders not really knowing what he was taking, but they were taking the discomfort away, so he was not bothered.

"I have concerns but I can see you have made your mind up and I will give you as much help as I can."

"I will need some things from your shop, if that is all right?"

"Take whatever you need, stock up well and be careful." Darius knew it was a stupid thing to say but he didn't know what else to say at this time, he was too nervous.

***

Xander stood tall and looked down at Chris on the bed, after suddenly entering the room and startling her. She looked up at the stabbing gaze he was giving her, saying nothing, merely returning his stare. She was not sure what was going to happen, so just kept her guard up.

"You are the entertainment for my guests and you will suffer much pain and tremendous torture. But we will have fun with you and we will have you over and over, just like we had your mother, Angelique, just like we had them all." His voice was calm and collected, but his tone was menacing and cold.

She swallowed and said nothing. She knew she had no chance of escape and listened to the words in her head that Ray had told her. Never give them an opportunity to beat you or harm you. Become nothing to them. If you mouth off, they will kick you to pieces and you will have no chance.

The house turned cold and Chris shivered she feeling it instantly. Sensing her thoughts, Xander smiled and seemed to smell the air.

"My guests are arriving," he said, turning and leaving the room.

Chris shook with the cold. She was nervous and agitated, so she stood and walked to the window, looking out across the fields once again. It was empty and deserted, no one near to help, no chance of escape and no knowledge of what was going to happen to her.

***

Xander looked at the smaller man in front of him. This man was dressed in a suit with a pencil moustache, narrow eyes and gaunt features. He looked evil and devious, which is exactly what he was.

"Have you really got her? Did you manage to capture her?" he asked Xander as he looked up at him and grinned a mischievous grin. He put his hands together in a gesture of glee and excitement he could not control.

"She is here, my friend, and, what is more, Kaden is dead."

"Are you sure? Did you see him destroyed? He has come back before. Did you take off his head?"

"Don't question me," Xander's voice became authoritative, "I have her in this house and we will take her tonight, we will all take her tonight, my friend."

"It will be a night to remember. Kaia is on her way and she is very excited, I know. She will be here very soon, Master, very soon, and she is looking forward to pleasing you." His manner was one of obedience but untrustworthy submissiveness.

"We have some very special friends coming, very special indeed. You go and prepare, I have something to attend to."

Xander walked out of the room and left the man standing next to the large open fireplace. He seemed to have something on his mind. He went to the back of the house to a room where an Ouija board was set out on a table. He put his large hand over the board and closed his eyes.

He lifted his head as he saw the farmhouse property where he had taken Chris from. Eyes still closed, he moved his hand over the board. He could see the lake, moving up, he saw the dead giant, moving his hand, he came closer to where the four fighters had destroyed Ray. He saw two dead and frowned, moving his hand a little further somewhat apprehensively. He saw the third laying dead, the fourth was laid out not too far away.

He scanned over the area again and again, trembling with anger. He could see no sign of Ray, his car or his beast. His hand became a clenched fist and he brought it down with a tremendous thud on the board shouting out, "No! Impossible!"

He opened his eyes and they were jet black, his eyebrows were arched and his eyes narrowed. His body shook with anger and he shouted out a cry that the whole house heard, shaking the building to its very foundations.

***

He was not the only one looking at a Ouija board. Ray was doing the same thing, asking for help from Kaden once again.

It was late afternoon and he had his car and his weaponry, and his will to fight was stronger than ever. He had taken the pills Jan gave him and he felt ready.

He was peering at the board as he used the wooden pointer and watched the board, trying to find out where Chris was and if he could get directions. He began to sweat as he stared intently at the board.

Nothing was happening, nothing was coming through to him. The board was still and blank. He lifted his hands and sighed, then he tried again, this time asking for Angelique's help. But again nothing happened.

He decided to go back to basics and do what he used to do. This board had, in the past, pinpointed witches for him. He used to follow its directions all over the country and it never let him down. He tried this and didn't ask anyone else except the board itself.

The pointer shook and he closed his eyes. He felt the energy just like the old days, the directions, the way he had to go. It was strong and powerful, more powerful than he had ever felt before. This must be it; nothing else could be generating so much energy and force.

Xander was always able to block this, but the people around him and the army he was gathering could not. They were emitting their evil; their dark forces were like a beacon to Ray's board and it homed in on them.

Ray began to see the large estate set in its own grounds and surrounded by fields. He saw the large mansion standing like a dark vision from the past, bleak and mysterious.

Built some centuries ago, it had been the home to Xander's family for many years. This is where he resides and this is where he rules from.

Ray had him at last and he knew it, he knew this is where Xander must be so, therefore, he knew it is where Chris must be. Unfortunately, the amount of evil force that was coming through was too great for him to take on alone, he knew it by the way the board shook and the amount of darkness he was seeing and evil he was feeling.

He pulled back his view and started to locate the general area. He did this as he used to; first, homing in on the evil showed him where it was, then he saw the area, then the direction. Suddenly he knew exactly where it was. He had him; he had Xander and he had his killing ground.

Ray backed off from the board and let go of the planchette and it felt like he was being unplugged from the mains. He breathed out loudly and the feeling he had in his body was electric; he had never felt such force before.

He looked around the room and saw Darius looking at him and Jan standing next to him. They both looked worried and waited for Ray to say something to them.

He composed himself for a moment and said to them, "I have him, I know where he is."

Both Darius and Jan held each other, gripped tight to each other's arm. They were scared stiff, but still wanted to help.

"Is he far, Ray? Where is he?"

"I have always felt this tremendous draw to Yorkshire all my life. Chris was right, there is a reason for it. The evil I have to destroy lives there. He is about two hours away and the force coming from that place is tremendous. I will not be able to take them on by myself."

"What do you want us to do?" Jan said, while Darius nodded, agreeing with the question.

"No, it's too dangerous. I could not ask you to…"

He was cut short by Darius who held his hand up saying, "Ray, listen to me. We are not fighters, we are a peaceful community. But you need help and I can get people to help you. Now, please, just say what you need and we will do our best. I have already talked to some men who are willing to fight with us, friends and fellow followers. We all know what you have done and we will all be proud to help you and Chris. We must get her safe and we must do it now."

Jan nodded and then added in a stern voice, "We are wasting time. If you have a plan, then tell us what it is. I want to get stuck in and help you." With that, she reached in her pocket and gave Ray two tablets, which he took without question.

"You don't understand, this is not a game. They will kill you, rip you apart and destroy your very soul," Ray said seriously.

"We are quite aware of them, much more than you give us credit for. Now stop pissing about and let's get going." Her strong attitude shocked Ray a little, but he liked her guts and courage. They were with him, whether he liked it or not.

"How many do we have and what are they willing to do?"

"Six men, good and strong, and they will fight because they know they are fighting evil. They are not as proficient as you, they are not warriors, but they have courage and commitment. They all know of you and are willing to help you. I have equipped them with weapons and they are on standby," Darius told him, sounding like a true soldier.

Ray could not help but feel proud and glad that he had such friends. He nodded and decided to do it. He knew he needed help and any help was better then none at all.

It was less than ten minutes later that Ray was standing outside, letting Bodie into his car. He noticed the mechanic come around the corner with two other men in a car. They got out and came over to Ray. This was half of his fighting force. They introduced themselves and seemed willing. As Ray was explaining what they will come up against, three more men walked up to them from the road.

His army was complete and Ray was briefing them the best he could, making them understand that it was not going to be easy.

Darius got into a large vehicle and the three men on foot got in also. Jan went with Ray, taking a hold all bag with her. They convoyed out onto the road and away, following Ray and all willing to fight the best they could. They were all frightened, but fortunately they had no time to think about it to much as it was all happening so fast. Their admiration for Ray and Chris carried them and their loyalty was never in question.

This was going to be a battle some of them may not return from. But they had accepted that and Ray had told them that if they can except that, then nothing will stop them. The fear will not get in their way and it will not hamper their judgment or strength.

He was proud of their bravery, he just hoped their enthusiasm carried onto the battlefield and they didn't turn and run at the last moment. He knew all too well that talking a fight is much different than actually fighting a fight.

Ray drove fast, knowing exactly where he was going, with the two other vehicles following him. Jan leaned down to her hold all and took out what Ray recognised straight away as a 9mm Browning automatic handgun.

He looked at her with surprise and she smiled back and said without any hesitation, "I was the target champion three years running in our club. Don't ask me where I got this because I am not supposed to have it. It has a magazine of thirteen rounds and, to be honest, will fire any nine millimetre round, but I have parabellum cartridge for it."

She took two spare magazines from her bag and placed them in the inside pocket of the leather jacket she was wearing, then she holstered the handgun in a shoulder holster she had under the jacket.

Ray was quietly impressed and said nothing about it. He was pleased she had such a weapon and knew how to use it. Again, his only concern was that shooting a target is not like shooting someone for real.

"What other weapons do we have?" Ray asked her, without taking his eyes off the road. He was travelling fast and didn't want to make any mistakes.

"Darius has his shotguns and the lads have crossbows and knives. I have my gun and this," she pulled a large bowie knife from her hold all bag. She held it up proudly and looked at the sharp, thick blade.

"Fucking hell, woman, what the hell are you doing with that?" Ray could not believe what he was seeing. Jan the silly girl-like woman doctor he thought he knew had just turned into a mercenary with the array of weapons in her bag.

"Do a lot of damage with this, Ray, thought it might come in handy. You can have it if you want."

"Thank you. Listen, Jan, I really do appreciate all your help, but you must understand when you come up against these things you have to act and do it fast. Any hesitation will be fatal. Can you point that gun at a person and pull the trigger without thinking twice? It is not like shooting a target, love, it takes a lot to do it and it makes one hell of a mess. It not like the movies with a little hole and a speck of blood, it is vicious and sickening."

"Don't worry about any of us. We will fight because we are fighting evil. I see them as a target, not a human being, that is how we all see it. They are vile creatures who need destroying. Not people, not humans, they are the devil's targets and that is why we will not let you down."

Ray was again impressed and a little more at ease, but not a lot. He would believe it when he saw it.

The drive did not take him two hours, he did it in about an hour and forty minutes. Finally reaching the area, he slowed down, seeing the place from his vantage point on the road.

He looked over and scanned the area all around it. Plenty of killing ground and open space. It wouldn't be easy to get near it undetected.

They all got out of their cars and stretched their legs. Bodie jumped out and scented and marked. Ray went to the back and got his binoculars out and took a closer look at the place.

He peered from his elevated position at the building, looking at each window and each door. He inspected the whole front of the large building. He dropped down the binoculars and said as Darius came up to him, "I am going to take a look around the side and back across those fields. Keep out of sight and keep your wits about you."

Ray was then gone, quickly moving along the road and into a small cluster of trees, with Bodie following him. Darius watched him go, quietly wishing him luck before going back to the cars to join his friends.

It took Ray only five minutes to circle the grounds and he was just below the horizon in the fields to the back. He lay down, blending into the ground as much as he could, then took the binoculars and moved the small centre wheel, focusing the glasses to a crisp clear image. He scanned the back of the house, which looked secure.

He moved his focus up to the window above the back door, seeing nothing. He moved to his right to the high second window and his mouth dropped open and bolt of emotion shot through him.

Right there, looking out over the fields, was Chris. He was zoomed right in on her. He looked at her sad face and sunken eyes. He wanted to stand and wave, he wanted to run and grab her, but he knew he couldn't. He just looked at her, grateful that she was alive. He stayed there too long but could not drop his gaze. Bodie stayed low and watched the house.

CHAPTER 21

Chris was looking far out across the fields. She moved her eyes across the horizon and back again when, suddenly, she stopped. She frowned slightly, wondering if her eyes were playing tricks. She put her hands up against the glass and peered out, trying to see as far as she could. Her breath misted the glass as she looked hard at what she thought she saw. Some movement and, yes, it was a dog and a man looking at the house. She could not make out clearly who it was but she knew in her heart it was him. She stood back, a grin on her face, and she waved both arms back and forth, signalling and hoping he saw her.

She could not control her excitement. Looking behind her to make sure she was alone first, she frantically waved and tried to signal him. Ray could see her through the binoculars and smiled. It lifted his heart and gave him strength. She was alive and now she knew he was too.

He got to one knee, signalled Bodie to leave and then turned to leave himself. He put his arm up to acknowledge he had seen her and then was gone.

Chris could not control herself. Ray was alive and he was here. She knew it was him, there was no mistaking it when he stood. It was Ray all right and he was coming for her. Her spirits lifted and she was excited.

She walked to the door and could feel the adrenaline rushing through her veins. The pain and the hurt and aches were gone, she wanted to fight and get out of here. Her man had come for her and she felt so good she could cry.

***

Ray was back with Darius about ten minutes later. He walked up to where they had parked off the road, a few yards from where he had left them.

"She is alive, I have just seen her in an upstairs window," Ray announced to them all. Their joy for her and him was obvious and they showed it openly.

"What is the plan, what are we going to do?" Jan asked, standing like a true professional with holstered gun and zipped up jacket.

"Well she saw me, so she has been alerted and will know what to do on the inside if she can. It looks like there is only one way in and out. I have a feeling there will be a lot of them in the place, there are a few cars parked at the front and I guess more will be on their way. It is no good me trying to sneak in, they will detect me straight away. I would go for a full frontal assault."

"Won't they see you coming?" the mechanic said.

"Xander will already know I am here. Now listen, no one try and go for him, he is much too powerful. I want you all to kill anything else you see. Don't be fooled by what they look like, man, woman, child or dog, just kill it. Nothing good is in that house except Chris."

"Don't worry, Ray, we all understand what must be done and we are with you," Darius said reassuringly.

"I hope so, because it will get bloody and messy. Do not let any of them get too close. If you see it, kill it without hesitation. If you hesitate, you're dead, simple as that. I will go for Xander and Chris."

"Be careful. How do you feel, have the tablets I gave you taken the pain away?" Jan asked him.

"Seem to have, yeah. Are they legal?"

She just smiled at him and handed him the large bowie knife. He took it and saw everyone else getting ready. Darius had a sawed off shotgun and a belt of cartridges around his shoulder. He knew Jan had her automatic and he saw the six men with crossbows, arrows and knives.

Darius reached into the back of his vehicle and pulled a shotgun out, which he threw to Ray, saying, "Winchester Ranger twelve gauge. A bit old, but it does the trick. You have four shells in the magazine, I'm afraid that is all I have for it."

Ray took the gun and knew what he was going to use it for straight away. He took one more look around and then made his decision. The warrior was switched on.

"Fight like fuck, show no mercy, and kill everything you see," he said to them as he got into his car, started the engine and closed the door. Bodie was already on the back seat and just as ready as his master was.

Ray put the shotgun across the front seat and the knife next to it. He was focused, ready and going into battle.

***

Chris could feel something was going to happen. She didn't know how, but she could feel it. She pounded on the door with all her might, shouting to let them know she had her voice back. She heard someone coming up the stairs and just hoped it was Skank.

The door flew open and, without losing a second, Chris lashed out hard at Skank's face as she opened the door. Chris punched her full in the face and sent her flying backwards to the floor.

Following her out and onto the landing, Chris jumped hard onto the chest of her victim and brought her full weight down, knocking the wind out of her. Kicking hard,

Chris aimed her shoe at the head of this woman and caught her perfectly across the temple.

Blood began to pour from the cut and she rolled over to try to get away, but Chris had not finished, she wanted to make sure this one was not going to get up. She pulled her long hair, lifting her head and ramming it down viciously into the floor and then again and again, smashing her face. Blood splattered out of her smashed nose and face, she was dazed and tried to stagger up but the force of the blows kept her there and she was down for the count.

Standing, Chris got her bearings. She dashed across the landing at the top of the stairs and looked down. She saw at least twelve witches dash to the door and then stop as they heard the shotgun fire.

Ray was on the other side of the door. He was firing at the hinges and lock on the door, blowing them clean off and kicking the door in. He moved back out of the way as the evil horde charged out.

The six men with crossbows were standing in a firing line and all let go at once. The arrows flew and hit their targets well, knocking six back to the ground instantly. Jan squeezed her trigger and hit her targets with ease, shooting straight for the chest, the largest target she had. She fired two rounds into each, knocking them backwards.

The rest of them froze and snarled, backing into the safety of the house again. Ray dashed in and Bodie followed, having already chosen his target, was pouncing onto it, teeth bared and ready. The witch had no chance, she was torn apart instantly.

Ray lifted the gun and fired the last shell off at two oncoming creatures. He hit one, the shotgun pellets peppering her back and knocking her down. The other kept coming, snorting at him like a wild boar. Ramming the barrel of the gun into its face, Ray

knocked it back and into his swing range. He flipped the gun around and swung it like a

baseball bat, knocking the witch's head awkwardly off to the side, forcing her body to

follow with the momentum.

Chris watched in amazement from her vantage point. She punched the air and

shouted 'Yeah' as Ray smashed the butt of the shotgun down onto the witch's head as she

lay on the floor, demolishing it into oblivion.

He looked up right into the eyes of his beloved Chris. She looked back, matching

his stare. They didn't say anything because they didn't have to; it would all be said later.

Chris ran down the stairs as Ray spun on his heels, hearing someone coming up

behind him. It was a tall woman with hands lifted like claws, her teeth bared and snarling.

He noticed the sound of gun shots again from outside and some sort of battle

going on out there, but his immediate problem was in front of him.

Bodie was fighting with a man who had appeared from the side door; he was

swiping a stick at Bodie but was no match for the large animal and it was only a matter of

time before he would be dead also.

Ray looked at the black eyes bearing down and trying to burn into him. She was

vicious and snarling at him with venom.

Chris started to move across the landing and a side door opened. The thin, creepy

man before was there, his narrow eyes looking at Chris, and he licked his lips in

anticipation. As Chris went past the door, he pounced on her with a grunt and devilish

laugh, swiping at her and knocking her down.

Unfortunately for him, he had underestimated his opponent. Chris rolled off to the side and was up with lightning speed, facing him and ready to fight. It shook him slightly

and his surprise and hesitation was all she needed to get the first blow in. She punched

him on the lower jaw, knocking him back with a snorting sound. He kicked out however

and caught her as she came dashing forward. His shoe sank deep into her stomach,

knocking her back. He pounced once again and they were in combat on the landing,

fighting dangerously close to the top of the stairs.

Ray pulled the large Bowie knife out slowly from his belt. He gripped the hard

wooden handle tight and held it ready. He had seen enough of these things to know when

they were about to attack or pounce. She circled him slowly, bobbing her head up and

down like some sort of serpent and hissing at him.

Ray was focused and was ready. She knew this and it caused her to wait and not

dash in. She knew when she was confronted with someone who was able to destroy her

and she was not going to do anything stupid. She circled and watched him.

Bodie had just finished bringing his man down and tore at his throat, leaving a

mass of blood on the floor. It was still dripping from his fangs when he came over and

growled at this woman.

She backed up and looked around; the odds were stacking up against her and she

didn't like it. Bodie and Ray had become a unit and she was nervous. Both Bodie and his

master moved and suddenly, before she knew what had happened, she was trapped

between them.

In desperation, she raced forward. Bodie pounced and Ray dashed in, both hitting

her at the same time. Bodie brought her down and Ray plunged the knife deep into her

and pulled it to the side, ripping her throat out. He lifted the knife and brought it down with both hands, stabbing it deep into her heart.

The thud and sound of cracking bone was loud, but it was overshadowed by her cries and the gurgling noise she made as the blood pumped out of her jugular and down into her lungs.

Ray was up and he spun around; he felt the presence before he saw him.

Chris kicked out and sent the creep flying back and down the stairs. He rolled down the staircase and sprawled out at the bottom unnaturally; his back had snapped and he was dead before he hit the bottom step.

She came down, freezing at the bottom of the stairs as she saw the large figure in front of Ray. It was Xander, looking calmly evil and ready. He looked up as Darius and the others all came running into the house where they all stood a few yards behind Ray, panting anxiously, their weapons up and pointing at him.

Chris stood next to Ray, who was staring into the two eyes that staring back at him. He gripped the knife and was ready. He wanted to get in and finish it, despite knowing that it was not going to be easy.

Xander looked unruffled and in control. He lifted his head and looked at each person in turn, slowly moving his eyes to each individual then back to Ray. His mouth opened as he snarled, his eyes narrowed and he let then out a cry so piercing that it hurt their ears.

"Hit him!" Ray shouted.

He threw his knife hard and true and it struck home, straight into Xander's chest.

The six crossbows let fly, each arrow embedding into Xander's body at various points. Jan aimed and fired her full magazine into his chest and the force knocked him backwards as the blood splattered. The arrows dug in deep and Ray's knife stuck out from a wound that should have been fatal.

Darius came forward and let his two barrels off, hitting Xander in the head and face. The pellets tore his flesh and disfigured his face, but still he did not go down.

Jan was dropping out the magazine and replacing it with another one. She again took aim and fired, this time hitting him in the head and neck. The 9mm cartridges flew true and hit their target perfectly; she was an excellent shot. But still he did not go down.

Blood and flesh was dripping from him. The hideous sight was disturbing and sickening to see, but Xander still stood and looked through the only eye he had left at Ray. His horrific injuries seemed to do nothing to stop him. He lifted his arms and shouted a spell in a deafening voice. He waved his arms and then stood silently.

It was Bodie who noticed, he was the first one to act. The dead man at the bottom of the stairs moved and stood up, the man with the stick that Bodie had killed was up and running into the fight, and the witches from outside were coming back to life and back into the house.

The dead were rising and Xander had control over them. The battle had to be fought again.

Bodie ran and jumped, bringing his man down. Chris turned and, once again, was fighting the creepy man. She picked up a metal poker from the fireplace and used this to lash out and stab at her attacker.

Jan was again firing into the oncoming witch. Darius doing the same, but it was having no effect. They could not be killed while Xander was controlling them.

In desperation, Ray ran and body shot Xander back and to the floor. The hand to hand fight was nasty and brutal, both men ripping into each other and tearing at anything they could. Ray fought like a mad man, biting and hitting and tearing.

Xander hit him back hard and was wreaking havoc on Ray. He was weak and not one hundred percent fit; the tablets that Jan had given him were good, but he could not put up with this punishment for long. His body was pain-ridden and weakening by the moment.

The fight in the hall was like nothing seen before. The carnage was extraordinary, but the witches would not die, could not die, not while Xander had the power over them, the power he had gained from the shifter. Ray was knocked back and he rolled over in excruciating pain.

"Bodie!" he shouted in desperation.

His faithful dog left the man he was fighting, turned and ran with full force at Xander. Ray stood screamed out through his pain and rammed forward at the same time. They both hit Xander full on, knocking him back once again. Bodie used his weight and power to topple him over and hold him down while Ray lifted his aching body over and took the knife from Xander's chest.

He pulled and twisted it out. Xander screamed and hit Bodie hard, tearing into him, but Bodie was in a frenzy and just savaged him, tearing, pulling, ripping and shaking his head with jaws full of flesh.

Ray took the knife and sliced it across Xander's throat, cutting deep. Again he did it, and again, cutting through the flesh and reaching the spinal column. He lifted the large blade and hacked it down onto the bone. Xander was striking him, but he could tell the power was leaving him and it gave Ray strength to carry on under the barrage of hits. He screamed out as he hacked the last bit of bone and sliced with the knife again, causing Xander's head to fall to the floor.

He had extinguished any chance of the evil man's survival, as far as he was concerned, and if this had not worked, he was finished.

Ray held the head as he rolled to his knees and stood, unsteady on his feet. He looked back at the carnage, with Bodie panting by his side. All the witches and attackers were dead and not even Xander had power left.

The ragtag warriors all looked at the blood-stained and exhausted Ray and Bodie. He looked over at each in turn and left his gaze finally on Chris, who was slowly walking towards him.

He stood, breathing heavily, gasping for breath. The room was silent. He looked down and lifted the shattered remains of Xander's head into the air. He then tossed it into the open fireplace and turned to Chris, who standing in front of him, staring into his eyes.

She could see he was still in a confused and dangerous state, he needed calming and bringing back down to reality. She waited for him to come down and get settled again. He put out his hand and touched her face.

"Let's get out of here, Ray," she said to him.

He simply nodded and she found it totally incredible that she was so calm at a time like this. She knew she had to be, though, and knew she had to get Ray out and fixed up once again. It was not the first time and most definitely would not be the last.

He walked out and Darius followed, as did the six men with crossbows. Jan watched as Ray walked past her. She had such a feeling of pride and admiration for him that she was near tears. Looking back, she scanned the hall and suddenly felt scared. The blood, the carnage, the bodies ripped to pieces on the floor, and the smell of evil was chilling. She shivered and turned and hurriedly left the room.

***

It was silent and still, the battlefield was quiet. Xander's body was motionless and his head in flames in the fireplace. Slowly and silently a door opened from the back of the hall. The second skank that Chris had seen walked slowly out and looked across the hall.

She turned as a tall figure came out behind her; good looking and very smartly dressed. He looked across the carnage in front of him and shook his head slowly as looked at Xander's body.

He turned and looked at his woman, who came next to him obediently and without hesitation, then he opened his mouth slightly and bared his fangs at her. His curled lip and two large protruding fangs made him look evil, which is exactly what he was.

Unnoticed by Ray and the others, they slipped out the back door and melted into the darkness

***

Chris was driving. Ray was laying on the back seat with Bodie, quietly nursing his wounds and trying to stay still, because his body jolted with pain if he moved. The adrenaline had gone and the hurt had taken its place.

Jan rode in the front seat with Chris and Darius followed with the six men. They drove steadily away down the road, convoying back to civilization. The stories and the explanations and the conversation would all come later, they had to get away get safely and get fixed up.

They had no idea what they had left behind, though they would find out later. Oblivious to it now, they drove away and out of the county, back to Darius's house. The time to mend, to heal and to forget had begun.

The End ………….. To be Continued with Shadows of Darkness